M WASHBURN
Washburn, L. J.
Killer on a hot tin roof /

KILLER

on a

HOT TIN
ROOF

Books by Livia J. Washburn

FRANKLY MY DEAR, I'M DEAD

HUCKLEBERRY FINISHED

KILLER ON A HOT TIN ROOF

Published by Kensington Publishing Corporation

KILLER
on a
HOT TIN
ROOF

LIVIA J. WASHBURN

KENSINGTON BOOKS
http://www.kensingtonbooks.com

KENSINGTON BOOKS are published by

Kensington Publishing Corp.
119 West 40th Street
New York, NY 10018

Library of Congress Card Catalogue Number: 2010934832

ISBN-13: 978-0-7582-2570-2
ISBN-10: 0-7582-2570-9

First Hardcover Printing: December 2010
10   9   8   7   6   5   4   3   2   1

Printed in the United States of America

This book is dedicated to my editor, Gary Goldstein,
my agent, Kim Lionetti, and of course,
to my muse, my husband, James Reasoner.

CHAPTER 1

Blanche DuBois was wrong: you can't depend on the kindness of strangers.

Not that I want to sound pessimistic, and let's face it, by the end of *A Streetcar Named Desire*, Blanche is more than a little nuts, anyway. But if you really want to be disillusioned about the human condition, try being a travel agent for a while.

I looked at the group of people gathered in the airport concourse and did my dead-level best not to shout, "Will all of y'all just shut up?"

Because that wouldn't have been professional, you see.

So instead I turned to Dr. Will Burke and said, "They're your colleagues. Can't you do something about them?"

He sighed. "I'll try. But remember, they're literature and theater professors. Drama comes naturally to them."

I'll say it did. At the rate they were going, I'd be a little surprised if we made it from Atlanta to New Orleans without some of them killing some of the others.

Unfortunately, given my track record with these literary-themed tours, that possibility wasn't as far-fetched as it sounds.

You may have read about me in the newspapers. Delilah Dickinson. Red-headed, with a temper to match (just don't remind me of it, if you know what's good for you). Divorced, approaching middle age too doggoned fast, owner of a semi-successful small business, a travel agency specializing in literary tours. I'd come up with the idea a couple of years earlier, after leaving a big agency to go out on my own, and, for the most part, it had worked out just fine.

I say for the most part because on a couple of tours, some pretty bad trouble had cropped up, and by bad trouble, I mean murder. Those cases had been solved and the killers caught—with some help from me, if I do say so myself—but naturally, the violence and scandal involved made folks remember them a lot better than they did the dozens of other tours I'd conducted that had gone off without a hitch.

You can't blame anybody for being interested in other people's troubles. It's part of the human condition, if you want to get all high-flown and philosophical about it. But the reputation those tragedies gave my agency made it an uphill struggle to keep things running in the black. I'd managed to do that, with a lot of help from my only two employees—my daughter, Melissa, and her husband, Luke—but it hadn't been easy.

Now I had a tour headed for another easy, the Big Easy, N'Awlins its own self . . . if we ever got off the ground.

Will held up his hands to get the attention of the approximately forty people who stood there with their carry-on bags around their feet. He was about my age, although his tousled blond hair gave him a bit of a boyish look. The glasses counteracted that by making him appear slightly professor-ish. We had dated off and on for a couple of years, ever since he'd found himself in the middle of my first tour—and first murder case—and I suspected it was because of his influence at the university that I was able to get the job of arranging to take this group of professors, spouses, and/or significant others to New Orleans for the annual Tennessee Williams Literary Festival.

You see, that's why I had Blanche DuBois on my mind.

The loud conversations that bordered on arguments were still going on. The members of the group didn't pay any attention to Will as he stood there waving his hands a little. He said, "Uh, excuse me, everyone?"

"You're gonna have to speak up," I told him. "Just pretend they're a bunch of unruly students in a lecture hall."

He glanced at me. "None of my students ever get that unruly. They pay attention to me. I give good lectures."

"Then pretend they're a bunch of third graders who're actin' up."

Will frowned. "I don't know how to do that."

I sighed and shook my head. I'd never been a teacher myself, but I had driven carpool plenty of times when Melissa was a kid.

"Hey! Y'all settle down, or I'll tell the pilot to go on to New Orleans without us!"

That shut 'em up. Of course, it might have offended them, too, but right then, I didn't care all that much.

An austere-looking man with white hair, glasses, and a wrinkled face stared at me and said, "I beg your pardon, Ms. Dickinson?"

I was about to apologize and explain why I'd yelled at them when it struck me how much he looked like Orville Redenbacher, the guy from the old popcorn commercials on TV. That made it hard to think of anything to say.

Will, bless his heart, jumped right in. "I think what Ms. Dickinson is trying to say, Dr. Jeffords, is that we all need to show a little more decorum. You know how it is with airports now. The extra security and all that."

"Oh." Dr. Jeffords blinked, then slowly nodded. "Oh, yes, of course."

That was pretty slick of Will, I thought. You can ask folks to

3

do almost anything in an airport now, and as long as you look properly solemn when you mention "the extra security and all that," they'll go along with it.

I put a smile on my face and said, "I just think you should save all these spirited discussions for the panels when you get to New Orleans, so the other people attending the festival can get the benefit of them, too."

Another man said, "But Dr. Paige claims that the hurdles on which Brick breaks his leg have no ethnological significance."

A slender, attractive woman in her mid-thirties, with short dark hair, gave what my mama would have called an unlady-like snort. "They're hurdles on a high school track," she said. "They have no ethnicity, so how can they have any ethnological significance? You might as well argue that they're gynocentric."

"Well, they could be," another man said. "If you consider Brick's obvious homosexuality and his later reaction to Maggie, the hurdles could be seen as a barrier over which Brick has to leap. When he fails to make that leap, when he fails to clear the threat of Maggie's sexuality, so to speak, or all female sexuality, as it were, then he's left a physical cripple—"

"He's disabled," yet another of the professors interrupted. "You can't say 'crippled.' He's physically disabled, which serves as a counterpoint to the emotional disability which he's already displayed by his incipient alcoholism, as well as his failure to reconcile his feelings toward Skipper—"

The man who had first brought up the hurdles said, "Yes, well, that line of argument merely reinforces my theory, which is never refuted in the text of the play, that Skipper was actually black, which again raises the issue of ethnological significance. The hurdle that Brick fails to clear is not his sexuality, but rather his racism!"

"Oh, surely you can't believe that!" the first prof said. "The

4

historical aberration alone is enough to discredit the entire idea. Brick and Skipper were roommates in college. A black man wouldn't have been attending the same college as Brick during that time period."

The first professor sniffed and sneered. "It's what the playwright meant, whether it's historically accurate or not."

Everybody started talking at once then. I looked at Will and asked, "Did you understand all that?"

He nodded and said, "Unfortunately, yes. And they're back at it again, aren't they?"

"Let 'em fuss," I said. "I don't guess it's doing any real harm, and at least I can count heads while they're busy arguin'."

When I had done that, I realized that there weren't forty of them after all. I only had thirty-eight members of the tour accounted for.

Two were missing.

"You know everybody who's supposed to be here, right?" I asked Will.

"I think so."

I held out the clipboard with the passenger list on it. "Then go through this and tell me who's not here yet." I glanced at the giant electronic bulletin board that showed all the arrivals and departures of the flights. Our flight to New Orleans was still supposed to be on time, which meant we had about ten minutes before the boarding call. Having a couple of missing tourists now was cutting it closer than I liked.

Will took the clipboard and started glancing back and forth between the list and the group of people gathered in front of us. I could tell he was checking them off in his mind.

After a minute or so, he handed the clipboard back to me and said, "The only ones who haven't shown up are Michael Frasier and whoever he's bringing with him."

I glanced down at the list, saw the lines that read "Dr. Michael Frasier" and "Guest of Dr. Michael Frasier." I'd been able to leave that second spot unspecified when I was booking the trip, although of course I'd need the name of whoever was accompanying Dr. Frasier, and the person would have to have ID before they would be allowed to board the plane. The airlines don't allow anybody on anymore without knowing who they are.

"You know this fella Frasier?"

"Of course," Will said. "Not well, mind you. He's only been at the university for a year or so. But I've met everyone in the English Department."

"Well, he and his wife had better show up soon, or they're gonna get left behind."

"I don't think it'll be his wife coming with him."

"His girlfriend, then, if he's not married. Or his mistress, if he is."

Will shook his head. "Not that, either."

"Oh," I said. "That's all right. Nobody cares about things like that these days."

"No, no, I don't know that he's gay," Will said. "I don't know that he's not. But I'm pretty sure he's not married, and I never heard anything about a girlfriend or a boyfriend. I'm not sure he has a social life. He's pretty consumed by his work. Publish or perish, you know."

I'd heard the phrase and vaguely understood it, but I'd never had any direct experience with it, being a travel agent instead of a professor.

Before I could say anything, Will went on with relief in his voice, "Here comes Dr. Frasier now."

He was looking along the concourse in the terminal. I followed the direction of his gaze and saw two men coming toward us. The one who had to be Dr. Frasier had an air of impatience about him as he carried both bags. He looked like he wanted to stride on ahead but had to hold himself back so he wouldn't walk off and leave his companion. Every few steps, he seemed to pull himself back.

The other man shuffled along at what would have to be a maddeningly slow pace to anyone who could walk normally. He bent forward slightly at the waist, and his back was humped with age. He wore a brown suit and tie over a white shirt. The shirt's collar was loose around his stringy neck. An old-fashioned brown fedora was on his head. His arms moved back and forth a little at his side as he walked, almost like a puppet's. He had to be at least eighty years old, probably more.

I leaned close to Will and said quietly, "Would it be too politically incorrect for me to say that if Frasier is gay, he has pretty odd taste in boyfriends?"

"Yes," Will said. "Anyway, maybe that's his grandfather."

That was possible. Frasier looked like he was about forty, or half the old guy's age, in other words. He was slender, with tightly curled dark hair touched here and there with gray. His suit had a slightly shabby look, sort of like the one the old man wore. The difference was that Frasier's suit looked like it was the best he could afford on his teaching salary, while the old man's looked like he had owned it for the past fifty years.

The others had started to notice Frasier and his companion, and evidently they were as puzzled as Will and I were, because they gradually fell silent. Dr. Paige, she of the short dark hair and somewhat more commonsense attitude, glared at Frasier with obvious dislike. Curious, I glanced at the list in my hand. Tamara was her first name. She didn't really look like a Tamara to me, but of course you can't always go by names. Although I've been told that I look just like a Delilah.

I was too impatient to wait while the two newcomers made

their way all along the lengthy concourse. I went around the group and hurried to meet them.

"Dr. Frasier?" I said as I approached. "I'm Delilah Dickinson, the leader of the tour."

Frasier nodded pleasantly enough. "It's nice to meet you, Ms. Dickinson. I'm sorry we're late." With an expression that was half smile, half grimace, he inclined his head toward his companion. "Howard can't move very fast these days."

"That's all right. They haven't announced the boarding call for our flight yet, so you're here in time. I do need your friend's name, though, and he'll have to have his ID ready at the gate."

Before Frasier could reply, the old man said in a loud, surprisingly clear voice with a strong Southern drawl, "My name is Howard Burleson, young woman. I can speak for myself. And I don't need any identification. I know who I am."

"I'm sorry, Mr. Burleson," I told him. "I didn't mean any offense. But you, uh, have to have ID to board the plane—"

"He's got it," Frasier broke in. "Or rather, I do. They gave it to me at the home when I checked him out. I have his driver's license and social security card. Will that be enough? You don't need a passport, do you?"

I was tempted to tell him that the last time I'd checked, Georgia and Louisiana were both still in the United States, but I decided there was no point in being a smart aleck. Also, it bothered me that the state would give somebody as feeble as Howard Burleson a driver's license. But I said, "That'll be fine. Is Mr. Burleson your . . . grandfather?"

Burleson waved a gnarled hand. "I'm no relation to the boy. I'm just his meal ticket to fame and fortune."

I had no idea what that meant and didn't really care. Frasier looked annoyed and I thought he was going to say something, but just then the announcement came over the loudspeaker that Flight 561 to New Orleans was now boarding at Gate 3.

"That's us," I said as I took a pen and crossed through "Guest of Dr. Michael Frasier" and printed "Howard Burleson" in the space above it. "If you'll join the others. . . . Have you already checked the rest of your luggage?"

Frasier hefted the two carry-ons. "This is all we have. The festival is only five days."

Only a man could go on a trip for five days and fit everything he needed into a carry-on.

But there was no point in saying that, either, so I just ushered the two of them toward the rest of the group. By now they had picked up their bags and were making their way toward Gate 3, along with everybody else who was taking that flight to New Orleans.

I gave Will a reassuring nod. Now that everybody was here, things would be all right. The professors had stopped arguing, and they looked like the low-key, intelligent, and, well, professorial bunch I'd expected them to be in the first place. From here on out, I told myself, everything would go smoothly.

That was when Howard Burleson said, "It's goin' to be wonderful to see New Orleans again. I just wish poor Tom could be there with us."

Dr. Paige said, "Tom?"

"Tom Williams, of course," Burleson said. "Or Tennessee, as he called himself."

Dr. Paige stopped in her tracks. "You knew Tennessee Williams?"

Burleson stopped, too, and looked at her, his leathery face creasing in a smile. He ignored the gentle tugs on the sleeve of his suit coat that Frasier was giving him and said, "Knew him? Tennessee Williams and I were lovers, young woman."

CHAPTER 2

That stopped everybody in their tracks. I didn't really blame them. I wasn't even a professor, and I was surprised by the old man's statement. Here they were, going off to a five-day literary festival honoring one of America's most distinguished playwrights, and Howard Burleson wanted them to believe that he had been intimate with that very playwright.

At the same time, I wanted to shoo the group back into motion. The loudspeakers had already announced that our flight was boarding, and we didn't have the luxury of standing around gawking at Burleson, no matter how outrageous the claim he had just made.

And maybe it wasn't really all that outrageous. Even though most of my knowledge about Tennessee Williams and his life came from the movies based on his plays, I knew that he had been gay and had been involved with a lot of different men in his life. If Burleson was eighty now, he would have been in his twenties during Williams's heyday as a playwright. He could have been young and good-looking and just the sort that Williams went for. I didn't know.

But I knew it would be a big hassle if we missed our flight, so I forced those thoughts out of my head and raised my voice to say, "We'd better move along, folks. We don't want that airplane leavin' without us."

Dr. Tamara Paige turned her head toward me and said, "You can't expect us to just . . . just . . ."

Frasier clamped a hand on the old man's arm and tugged him toward the gate. "Not another word, Howard," he warned. "Do you understand me?"

I didn't like the browbeating tone that Frasier took with Burleson, but the old man just nodded and said, "All right, Doctor."

"What are you up to, Frasier?" Dr. Paige snapped.

"Be there when I present my paper," Frasier said. "You'll see." He steered Burleson toward the gate, and the others followed along behind them, chattering again now.

The routine of getting on the plane quieted them down. I spend a lot of time in airports, and even when you're an experienced traveler like I am, all the rigamarole can't help but remind you of why the extra precautions are in place. A lot of people still turn solemn when they get on or off a plane.

I took advantage of the opportunity to lean close to Will Burke as we were waiting to board and ask, "Do you believe that?"

"You mean do I believe what Mr. Burleson said about being Tennessee Williams's lover? Or that Frasier would drag him to this conference?"

"Actually, I was speakin' more in general, like you might say, 'Well, what do you know about that?' But I'd take an answer to either of the questions you asked."

"I have no idea whether Mr. Burleson is telling the truth," Will said. "It's not like we have a list of everybody Williams was involved with. We know the most significant ones, like Frank Merlo, but there were plenty of others."

I looked at the pink flush spreading across Will's face. "Why, Will Burke, you're blushin'," I said in surprise.

"I was raised in a pretty strict environment in a little Georgia town," he said. "There were more things going on in the world than I really knew about until I got to college."

Once I stopped to think about it, I knew what he meant. We get bombarded by so much all the time these days, we forget that there are still plenty of folks walking around who didn't have the Internet and cable TV when they were growing up. I should know, I'm one of them. Especially in rural areas, there were some things you just didn't see very often, so you didn't think about them all that much. Like Will said, you had to get out into the world before you started forming opinions, and even then, it was hard to escape your upbringings.

"Anyway," Will went on, "I'm not surprised that Frasier dug him out of the woodwork somewhere, or that he's taking Burleson to the festival. Like I said, he's all wrapped up in his work, and if what he says is true, it might be the basis for a good paper."

"And that's important to his career?"

He nodded. "Really important."

"Are you going to, what do you call it, give a paper at the festival?" I hadn't really had a chance to talk to Will about his schedule over the next few days.

"Present a paper. And no, not this year, although I have presented papers at the Williams Festival before. I'm just on some panels this year."

"I'll try to attend some of them," I promised . . . although if the panelists started in on that ethnological, gynocentric, English professor gobbledygook, I wasn't sure I'd know what they were talking about.

Will and I were the last ones in our group to board the

plane. We found our seats—I'd made sure they were together, of course—and settled back for the ride, which would only take a little more than an hour. As soon as the plane was in the air and it was all right to get up and move around, I unfastened my seat belt and started up the aisle to check on my clients and see that they were all settled in okay.

When I came to Dr. Frasier and Howard Burleson, I stopped and asked, "How're you folks doin'? That take-off bother you any, Mr. Burleson?"

"Not a blessed bit. I have been on an airplane before, you know. I was quite the world traveler in my time." He had taken off his hat and held it precisely squared in his lap, revealing a mostly bald, liver-spotted scalp that had just a few strands of white hair draped over it. "Matter of fact, it was in Italy where I first met Tom. Venice is such a romantic city, you know."

Frasier put a hand on his arm. "I told you, Howard, save it for the conference."

"Very well," Burleson said. "The memories are quite clear, though, of the sun on the canals and the warm breeze blowin' through my hair."

"Yes, fine," Frasier said, obviously trying to suppress the impatience he felt. "You can tell everyone about it when we get to New Orleans."

I heard a snort from one of the seats ahead of them, and when I looked in that direction, I saw the close-cropped hair of Dr. Tamara Paige. She hadn't looked around, but I knew she could hear what Frasier and Burleson were saying and figured there was a good chance the snort had come from her.

"Where is it we're goin' again?" Burleson asked.

"New Orleans," Frasier said. "I've told you several times now, Howard."

"Oh, yes. New Orleans." Burleson sighed. "The French

Quarter. Such wonderful memories. I can see it all like it was just yesterday I was there."

I wondered if Burleson might have a touch of Alzheimer's. He seemed a little fuzzy about what was going on in the present, but evidently his memories of the distant past were crystal clear.

Of course, my memory wasn't what it once was, either. Age and trying to juggle too many things will do that to a person.

I moved on along the aisle and stopped next to two more seats that contained a man and a woman. She was a blonde in her thirties, pretty except for the fact that her jaw was maybe a little too wide for her face. The fella with her was older, maybe fifty, with thinning dark hair and broad shoulders that strained the sports jacket he wore. He didn't look like a professor to me. I know that's stereotyping, but he just didn't.

"Hello," I said. "I'm Delilah Dickinson—"

"We know," the woman said, smiling brightly up at me. That broad jaw accommodated a lot of white teeth. "I'm Dr. Callie Madison, and this is my husband, Jake."

"Hello," he said, not exactly surly but not all that friendly, either.

"Thank you so much for setting up this tour," Dr. Madison went on. "I've been to the festival before, of course, but never with a group like this. I understand that we're going to be seeing some of the other sights in New Orleans while we're there."

"Well, sure," I said. "Didn't you do that when you went to the festival before?"

"No, I always had to get back as soon as possible." She turned her smile on her husband. "Somebody has to take care of this big lug here."

I tried to think how long it had been since I'd heard anybody call somebody else a "big lug," but gave up after a second, when I couldn't remember. Instead I asked, "Are you interested in Tennessee Williams, too, Mr. Madison?"

He grunted. "Not really. I'm not much on plays and things like that. But Callie convinced me that this would be a good vacation for us."

He didn't sound to me like she had completely convinced him.

"And I've always wanted to try some of that food they have there," he went on, getting a little more animated now. "I want to go to that fat guy's restaurant."

"Paul Prudhomme," Callie said.

"Yeah, him. That fat guy. I like that Cajun stuff."

"Well, you're goin' to the right place, then," I told him. "New Orleans has some of the best Cajun cooking in the world."

Jake Madison nodded. "We'll see about that."

His wife rested her hand on his. "Surely you want to do more in New Orleans than just eat, Jake."

"I might take in some of that Dixieland jazz, too. 'When the Saints Go Marching In' and all that."

"And you'll come see me present my paper on Williams's use of imagery in *Suddenly, Last Summer*?"

"What? Oh, yeah, sure. Last summer. Can't wait."

I felt the growing strain in the air and thought that I might be contributing to it, so I figured I'd better move on. I said, "If there's anything I can do for you folks to make y'all's trip better, you just let me know."

Callie turned that hundred-watt smile on me again. "Oh, we certainly will."

I wondered how much cajoling it had taken for her to get her husband to come along with her on this trip. Quite a bit, I suspected. Without the Cajun food and the saints marching in, I wasn't sure if Jake Madison would have ever agreed.

Dr. Paige was sitting next to Dr. Jeffords in the next pair of seats. She was in the aisle and he was next to the window. She looked up and gave me a curt nod, but Dr. Jeffords, the one who looked like Orville Redenbacher to me, was friendlier.

"I'd say we're off to a good start, wouldn't you, Ms. Dickinson?"

"We're all here, we left on time, and the plane didn't crash on take-off. Three for three."

He laughed. "That's a rather fatalistic way to look at it, but I suppose you're right."

"Are the two of you looking forward to the festival?"

Dr. Paige said, "I was . . . until I realized that it's liable to turn into a sideshow, rather than a serious literary conference."

Dr. Jeffords frowned and leaned toward her. "Now, Tamara—"

"You're the head of the English Department, Andrew," she said. "You must have known about this ridiculous stunt that Frasier's trying to pull."

"As a matter of fact, I didn't." A crisp note edged into his voice. "Dr. Frasier didn't have to clear his presentation with me. You could take it up with the festival organizers, though. I'm sure he had to submit an abstract of his paper to them for approval before it was placed on the program."

Dr. Paige gave a little shake of her head. "It's not worth the trouble. Let him go ahead and make a fool of himself. He'll never be allowed to present again."

"But what if he has something worthwhile to say? Shouldn't we give him the benefit of the doubt?"

"You think that old man was really some cabana boy that Williams picked up?"

"I don't have any proof that he's not," Jeffords said.

That made Dr. Paige frown. She couldn't disprove Burleson's claim, at least not at this point, because she didn't even know the details of it. She'd have to attend Frasier's presentation for that.

Me, I didn't give a hoot 'n' holler one way or the other. I just wanted to shepherd this bunch to New Orleans and then get 'em all back home safely to Georgia. If I did that, it would be a good trip.

"I'll see y'all later," I told them. "If you need anything, you let me know. That's what I'm here for."

Two of the professors who'd been arguing in the airport terminal were sitting in front of Drs. Paige and Jeffords. I paused beside them, but they didn't look up at me. They were still going at it, each one trying to talk over the other. I heard the words "anthropomorphism," "epistemological," and "phallophobia" and decided it was better just to move on.

The next pair of seats held only one passenger, but he was a big one. I recalled that somebody in the group had paid for two seats, and this fella had to be the one. He had a round face, graying brown hair, balding at that, and a grayish-brown goatee. His shirt gapped a little between buttons because of the pressure that the massive belly put on it. Whoever said fat men were jolly got it wrong, at least in this case. He wore a pained scowl.

I leaned over him. "You need something, sir?"

"You're not a stewardess, are you?"

I didn't bother correcting him on his choice of terminology. I just said, "No, I'm Delilah Dickinson. I'm the tour director."

"Well, there's nothin' wrong with me that a good stiff drink won't fix. Why don't you go see if you can get me one of those little bottles of booze?"

I tried not to bristle, but like I said, I've got a temper, so it wasn't easy. I managed to smile and said, "I'll speak to the flight attendant."

A woman sitting in front of the man turned around in her seat and said, "No, you won't. He's not allowed to drink."

"Now, damn it, Junebug—" the big man began.

"Don't you Junebug me, Papa Larry. Edgar and I are just trying to see to it that you take care of yourself, and you know the doctor said you can't drink anymore."

A rumble came from the big man. I swear, it sounded almost like a big dog growling. "How'm I supposed to feel better if I can't drink? Do you know what this is gonna do to my creative juices?"

"I know what whiskey will do to your belly," the woman he'd called Junebug said. She didn't look like a june bug to me. She had a narrow face with short, wispy brown hair around it. "It'll burn out what little of the stomach lining you have left, and then you'll die," she went on.

"You don't know that," he said in a sullen voice.

"I know what the doctor said. I was there." She elbowed the man sitting beside her, who had an open laptop computer balanced on his thighs. "Tell him, Edgar."

The man didn't seem to want to tear his attention away from whatever he was doing on the screen, but he turned his head long enough to say, "June's right, Dad. No booze for you."

The big man settled back against the two seats and glared. "What the hell kind of a trip is this?" he muttered.

"It'll be a good one," I said, trying to sound optimistic.

He just gave a disgusted snort and looked out the window.

"Don't mind that old grump," Junebug said to me when I stepped up alongside the seats where she and her husband sat. "He ought to be happy. He's going to direct a performance of three of Williams's one-act plays. It's very prestigious to be asked to do something like that at this festival."

19

"I expect it is," I agreed. "I'm Delilah Dickinson."

She held out a hand to me. "Dr. June Powers." She nodded toward the man beside her. "This is my husband, Dr. Edgar Powers."

He didn't look up at me. His attention was fixed on his computer screen again. But he lifted a hand and said, "Hi."

"Glad to meet you, Doctor," I said.

"And you met my father-in-law, Dr. Lawrence Powers. He's one of the most esteemed theater directors and teachers of drama in the country."

I'd never heard of him, but I was willing to take her word for it. "All of you teach together at the university?"

"That's right. Well, we're in different departments. I teach American Literature, and Edgar's in . . . engineering."

I caught the little hesitation, as if she were slightly ashamed to admit that her husband was in the sciences rather than the arts. Every family has its dirty little secrets, I suppose.

"Well, if y'all need anything, you let me know, hear?"

I was about to move on when Dr. Lawrence Powers, a.k.a. Papa Larry, said, "Get me a drink and there's twenty bucks in it for you, Red."

I swung around toward him. I don't like being called Red any more than I like somebody commenting on my temper because I have red hair. But before I could say anything, I realized that Will was there. He must have come up behind me in time to hear what Powers said. He knew me well enough that he got between me and Powers with a slick little move that kept me from saying anything.

"Larry, it's good to see you again," he said. "June, Edgar, a pleasure as always."

Junebug simpered a little. That's the only way to put it. I

wondered if she might have a little crush on Will. I didn't figure I had any reason to be jealous, though. Edgar just grunted.

And I moved on to talk to the other members of the tour group, thinking that if anybody else called me Red or used the word "phallophobic," they might wind up having to call the sky marshal on me.

CHAPTER 3

For about a quarter of a century, the Tennessee Williams Literary Festival has been held every year in New Orleans, and while the scope of it has expanded somewhat to include other New Orleans–based literature and Southern literature in general, the focus is still on Thomas Lanier Williams and his plays, short stories, poetry, and novels, as well as how various aspects of his life influenced his work.

I'd done some research on him before starting the tour, as I always do. I consider myself a reasonably well-read person, but I suspect most folks know Willliams not from actually reading his plays but from seeing them performed, either on stage or on the screen. Women remember Paul Newman's blue eyes and brooding intensity as Brick; men remember Elizabeth Taylor walking around in that slip as Maggie the Cat. And I suspect that a lot of guys of a certain age, at some point in their life, have bellowed, "Stella!"

These things and a lot of others from Williams's plays, like that "kindness of strangers" line, have worked their way into the collective consciousness, to use a phrase that proves I'd been spending too much time around professors, especially a certain professor. Will always listened when I talked about the tour business, though, so I figured I ought to pay attention when he talked about academic matters.

Anyway, to get back to the festival, after an opening night reception and ceremony, it was four days of panel discussions, paper presentations, theater performances, readings, and some things that were more just for fun, like dinners and musical performances. Professors like to cut loose and let their hair down, too, I suppose, although I'd never been around a bunch of them actually doing that. I figured that might prove to be interesting, although I didn't really expect anybody to get out of line.

I had a charter bus waiting to take us from the airport to the St. Emilion Hotel—in the French Quarter, right around the corner from Bourbon Street—which was serving as the headquarters hotel for the festival. As the bus pulled up in front of the lovely old three-story building with its wrought-iron railings along the balconies, I felt the elegance and charm practically oozing from it. The French Quarter, more than any other part of New Orleans, had fully rebounded from the devastating tragedy of Hurricane Katrina several years earlier. That wasn't surprising, of course, since the French Quarter represented more tourist dollars than any other part of the city. I don't mean that to sound cynical. It's just a fact of life.

As the bus came to a stop, I stood up from my seat just behind the driver, turned to face the passengers, and raised my voice. "All right, folks, this is the St. Emilion Hotel. This is where we'll be staying for the next five nights. I think you'll be very pleased with your accommodations. The St. Emilion is one of the nicest hotels in New Orleans, which means it's one of the nicest hotels anywhere in the world."

It was expensive, too, but the group rates made it at least somewhat affordable. The university was probably picking up some of the tab for the professors, too, but that wasn't really my concern. Will and I got off the bus and I asked him to let the concierge know that we were here while I supervised the unloading.

That proved to be an unnecessary request. Before Will could even get through the big fancy wooden doors, they swung open and a whole squad of uniformed porters marched out to take over the bags and see that everybody got inside. A short, dapper black man in an expensive suit came out, too, spotted me, and crossed the narrow sidewalk toward me.

"Ms. Dickinson?"

"That's right."

"I'm Dale Gillette, the assistant manager of the hotel. I want to welcome you and your group to the St. Emilion and let you know that everyone on the hotel staff is dedicated to making your stay as pleasant and memorable as possible."

"That's mighty nice of you," I said. "It looks like you've sure got everything under control." Escorted by the uniformed porters, my clients were going inside to check in.

Of course, not everything could go smoothly. Sometimes I think it's a law of the universe. I heard a raised voice say, "No!" and turned to see Dr. Michael Frasier clutching one of the carry-on bags to his chest like it contained some sort of treasure.

"I said I'll take it," he told the porter who obviously had reached for the bag. "Just leave it alone."

The porter looked confused, and so did Howard Burleson, who stood next to Frasier. The porter said, "Of course, sir. I was just trying to help. I meant no offense. If you'd like to carry that bag, it's fine."

"Of course it's fine," Frasier snapped. "It's my bag."

Burleson raised a gnarled finger. "Actually, Doctor, I believe it's mine."

"It doesn't matter. I'm carrying it."

I didn't have any idea what the old man could have in his bag that would get Frasier so worked up. Some of the other members of the group were starting to look around at him, though, and I didn't want the scene he was making to get any bigger than it already was. I was about to try to smooth things over when Dale Gillette beat me to the punch.

The hotel's assistant manager stepped forward and motioned the porter back. He said, "Allow me to expedite the check-in process for you, sir. If you'll just come with me to my office, you won't have to stop at the desk. We'll see to it that you get right up to your room without any delays."

The offer of special treatment seemed to mollify Frasier. He nodded and said, "All right. Mr. Burleson has to come with me, though."

"Of course," Gillette murmured.

"I can't let him out of my sight," Frasier added.

"I understand," Gillette said without hesitation, even though he almost certainly didn't. He just wanted to get Frasier to shut up and get into the hotel. Since I wanted the same thing, I was more than happy to let Gillette coddle him.

The three of them went into the hotel through a side door that Gillette opened. Burleson couldn't muster more than a shuffle, so it took a few moments.

"That doesn't seem fair," somebody said in disapproving tones. I turned and saw Dr. Tamara Paige glaring at Frasier and Burleson as they disappeared into the hotel with Dale Gillette. She went on: "Frasier acts like a total jerk and then gets special treatment because of it."

"I agree with you," I told her. "It's not fair. But the assistant manager of the hotel wanted to do something to help, and I didn't want to make things worse."

"Then you should have left that blowhard and the old fraud back in Atlanta."

I pointed out the same thing Dr. Jeffords had earlier. "We don't know that Mr. Burleson's a fraud. He seems like a sweet old man to me."

Dr. Paige frowned. "It doesn't matter how sweet he is. He's still lying. And everyone at the festival will realize that when Frasier trots him out and tries to pass him off as something he's not."

I didn't see how she could be so sure about that. I was beginning to get the impression that if Dr. Michael Frasier said "up," Dr. Tamara Paige was going to say "down." I had seen situations like that before, where anything one person said or did was wrong, according to one particular other person. I knew what the reason for that attitude usually was, too.

So I didn't say anything else to Dr. Paige. I went over to Will instead and asked quietly, "Dr. Frasier and Dr. Paige . . . they used to be an item, didn't they?"

He frowned and said, equally quietly, "I don't like to gossip—"

"Sure you do," I broke in. "Everybody likes to gossip, even professors."

His frown went away and a faint smile replaced it. "Maybe *especially* professors. Academia is fraught with passion, intrigue, and drama."

"Uh-huh. Sort of like a Tennessee Williams play. What about Frasier and Paige?"

Will shrugged. "There were rumors, not long after he came to the university. . . . If they were involved, though, it didn't last for long. And, I suspect, from the hostility that's existed between the two of them ever since, that it didn't end well."

"You know which one of 'em broke up with the other?"

Will shook his head. "Not a clue."

"When it comes to men and women, it's always a little like junior high, isn't it, even at a university?"

"Maybe even more so."

"Yeah. The place is fraught."

He grinned and said, "Everybody else is inside. Maybe we'd better get checked in, too."

That sounded like a good idea to me. All the luggage had been toted in, and we were the last ones on the sidewalk. I thanked the bus driver and tipped him. We were supposed to have a bus to take us back to the airport the day after the festival ended, but it might not have the same driver.

As Will and I stepped into the hotel lobby a moment later, its opulence almost overwhelmed me. To begin with, the floors were polished marble in some places and polished wood in others, and the shine would almost blind you. What kept it from casting a glare over the whole place were the thick, gorgeous rugs that were placed here and there where heavy, overstuffed armchairs and sofas were arranged in conversation pits.

Then there were the vaulted ceilings, the crystal chandeliers, the potted palms, the beautiful paintings on the walls, and the slowly revolving ceiling fans with teak blades. The long registration desk was topped with the same marble that could be found in the floor. Music played softly from hidden speakers, and the air was crisp and cool and dry, as if the humidity from the street outside wouldn't dare try to come in here.

The registration desk was to the right of the lobby, a restaurant and bar to the left. Straight ahead lay a short, broad, marble-floored corridor where the elevators were located, and when I looked along it, I saw an indoor garden at the far end, surrounded by an atrium. I knew from studying the hotel's website that each room on the second and third floors had a private balcony overlooking that garden. The rooms were accessed from hallways that ran around the outside of the hotel, rather than from the atrium. A massive stained-glass skylight cast shifting patterns of color over the lush plants in the garden.

Will let out a low whistle. "Fancy," he said. "I'm glad the university is paying part of the cost for this, or else I'd never be able to afford it."

I didn't tell him that he was echoing the same thought I'd had a few minutes earlier. I just linked arms with him as we went over to the registration desk. Several of the professors were still checking in, but as Will and I walked up, one of them finished and the clerk looked past him at us, and asked, "May I help you?"

The professor was still standing at the marble-topped counter. As he turned away, he nodded to Will and said, "Dr. Burke."

Will returned the nod. "Dr. Keller."

The professor was a bulky, sort of sloppy man with a fringe of dark hair around a mostly bald head. He reminded me of Jake Madison in that if I'd seen him on the street, I never would have taken him for a professor. That would have been right in Madison's case but obviously not in Keller's.

I looked after him as he crossed the lobby toward the bank of elevators, and said quietly to Will, "Are you sure he's not like a Teamster boss or something?"

Will laughed. "Ian Keller is one of the foremost authorities in the world on American literature, with an emphasis on Southern authors of the twentieth century. He's written books on Faulkner, Flannery O'Connor, Carson McCullers, and Tennessee Williams himself."

"Okay. He looks more like a gangster to me."

"I've never heard anyone who has a bad word to say about him. He's brilliant."

"I'll take your word for it," I said. "His books would probably be over my head."

"Don't sell yourself short, Delilah," Will said. "You're one of the smartest people I know. Some of these people couldn't find their way out of a paper bag without a syllabus to guide them. You've got more sense than they ever will. Plus, you can solve murders."

I shook my head. "Bite your tongue. My murder solvin' days are over."

We stepped up to the desk. I told the clerk my name and Will's name, and within a couple of minutes we had the keys to our rooms, which were both on the third floor. A porter was standing by with a rolling cart that had our bags on it. He followed us to the elevators.

It had been a pretty easy trip so far, a little friction here and there, but nothing serious. You get some of that on any tour. You can't put several dozen people together for four or five days and have all of them get along all the time. And with a group like this, where everybody knew everybody else, it was even more likely that there would be a spat here and there, like the sharp comments that Drs. Frasier and Paige had tossed back and forth about each other like darts. Strangers would at least try to be on their best behavior around each other.

"You're going to the opening reception this evening, right?" Will asked me as we walked along the third floor corridor toward our rooms. Our feet sunk so deep into the plush carpet on the floor that I wasn't sure how the porter was able to wheel the luggage cart through it.

"Yeah, I'll be there," I told him. I had an all-access pass that would get me into any of the festival events, since I didn't know where I might be called upon to take care of the needs of my clients, but I planned to attend the panels Will was on if I could. Beyond that, I hadn't figured out which of the events I would attend. I hadn't even had a chance to study the schedule all that much. I wasn't a scholar, though, so I figured I would avoid the day-long roundtable discussion of Williams and his work, whether Will was part of it or not.

But a fancy cocktail reception followed by informal readings by the several well-known stage actors who were part of the festival . . . I figured I was up for that.

"Good," Will said. "We can have dinner first, or a late supper, if you'd prefer."

"Why don't we make it supper?" I suggested. "I know a little café not far from here that's good."

"All right. You know the French Quarter fairly well, don't you?"

"I've brought tour groups to New Orleans before," I said, "just not to this literary festival."

"And I've been to the festival but never really explored the French Quarter all that much. We can combine our experiences."

"Yeah, that's sort of what I had in mind."

"What's this café like?"

"Oh, you know, good food, dim lighting, soft music."

Will smiled. "Sounds romantic."

"Well, you heard what Howard Burleson said about what a romantic city New Orleans is."

"Are we going to find out if he's right?"

"We just might," I said.

CHAPTER 4

I wouldn't go so far as to say that the hotel room floored me when I went inside. After all, I've stayed in some pretty nice places in my life. But the room at the St. Emilion was right up there. Boy, was it ever.

The ankle-deep carpet continued from the hallway. It was the color of coffee with a lot of milk in it, slightly darker then the walls. A green, richly upholstered sofa and two chairs sat on three sides of a massive mahogany coffee table with a section of inlaid glass. Against one wall was an antique rolltop desk. Across from it was an old-fashioned writing table, although there was nothing old-fashioned about the high-speed Internet connection built into the wall above the table. A heavy, straight-backed chair with a cushioned seat and beautiful woodwork was pushed up to the table. Those furnishings were mighty nice.

The bed put them to shame.

It was a four-poster with an elegant canopy trimmed with lace and a spread of dark gold silk. Even though I knew it was a standard king-size bed, it looked enormous to me. What seemed like a dozen fluffy pillows were piled at the head of it. I felt a strong urge to dive right in the middle of them. The little kid in me experienced an even stronger impulse. I wanted to climb onto the bed and jump up and down. I didn't do either of those things, of course. I mean, the porter was unloading my bags from the luggage cart, and Will Burke was still standing there in the hall, watching me take it all in.

If they hadn't been there, there's no tellin' what I might have done.

As it was, I walked slowly across the room toward the curtained French doors that led out onto the room's private balcony overlooking the garden in the atrium. The curtains were already open part of the way. I thrust them back even more and stepped up close to the doors so I could see out. Wrought-iron tables with colorful umbrellas attached to them were scattered through the garden. The plants were so thick that if you were sitting at one of those tables, it might seem like you were alone in the middle of a jungle, unable to see anyone else. White-jacketed waiters moved discreetly from table to table, delivering drinks from the bar. It would be a wonderful place to have a private conversation, shielded from view by the profusion of plants around you and the brightly colored umbrellas above so that people on their balconies couldn't look down and see you.

I wondered what it would be like to share a bottle of wine with Will in one of those little hideaways. Maybe I would find out before the festival was over, I thought.

The only feature that struck me as being somewhat out of place in the room was the huge mahogany entertainment center with the 42-inch plasma TV in it. The remote control lay on the bed and had so many buttons you could imagine using it to launch the space shuttle. As I turned away from the balcony, I picked up the remote control and stashed it in the cabinet next to the TV, then closed the doors. There, I thought, that looked better. Now it might almost be an old-fashioned

34

wardrobe. Everything about the St. Emilion put me in an old-fashioned mood.

"What do you think?" Will asked from the doorway.

"It's beautiful," I said as I tipped the porter, who had finished carrying in my bags.

"Is this what my room will look like?"

"I doubt it. Every room here is supposed to be different. No cookie-cutter designs in the St. Emilion."

"I suppose I'd better go see." He paused. "You want to come with me and check it out?"

"Maybe later. I'm a little tired after the flight." Actually, I was dying to try out that mattress.

"Okay." Will smiled. "See you later." He started to turn away, then stopped again. "Should we meet down in the lobby and go to the reception together?"

"That sounds fine," I told him.

It was about four o'clock now, and the reception started at seven at the theater where the performances would be held during the festival. The theater was in walking distance of the hotel, only about three blocks away. Everything was close to everything else in the French Quarter.

"I'll see you down there at six-thirty," I went on. Actually, now that I thought about it, I was a little tired, and it might be a good idea to try out that mattress for real and catch a nap. If Will and I had that late supper, I might not get back to bed until after midnight.

And for that matter, I thought, once I did get to bed, I might not be going to sleep right away . . .

"All right," he said. "Six-thirty. I'll see you then."

With a little wave, he went on down the hall with the porter and the luggage cart. I closed the door, leaned against it for a second, and then turned back toward the bed.

"Mattress," I said as I kicked my shoes off, "here I come."

* * *

I wore a white-trimmed dark blue dress with a matching jacket and white heels, and a single strand of pearls around my neck, going for simplicity and elegance. What took the longest getting ready for the night was pinning up my unruly red hair into a partial updo. I knew that I cleaned up pretty good, as we say back home. Pretty good wasn't enough for tonight, though. In addition to Tennessee Williams scholars from around the country, there would be the movers and shakers of New Orleans high society in attendance, along with folks from Broadway and Hollywood.

Judging by the look on Will's face as I walked toward him across the lobby, I'd done all right. He was smart enough to know not to gush about how good I looked as I came up to him, because that would have implied that I didn't look all that good normally. But he was definitely impressed. He went for simple, too, saying, "You look beautiful, Delilah."

"Thank you, kind sir." He wore a black suit and a charcoal tie, and his hair was neatly styled for a change, and as I looked him over, I went ahead and used the line I had thought about earlier. "You clean up pretty good, too, Doctor."

He grinned. "Thanks. I'll admit I don't like dressing up very much, but I don't mind when the occasion warrants it. And I'd say it's definitely justified when I'm going out for an evening in New Orleans with Delilah Dickinson."

I linked my arm with his and said, "Honey, you just lead the way."

I had spotted several other members of the tour group in the lobby, and as we left the hotel I saw more of them walking along the narrow sidewalk. Night had fallen, but the streets of the French Quarter were brightly lit with gas lamps on iron posts along with the light that came through the windows of the nearby buildings. The area wasn't nearly as crowded as it is during Mardi Gras, of course, but there were still a lot of people making their way along the sidewalks. Some of them were pretty disreputable-looking characters, too, because, after all, what would the French Quarter be without some lowlifes? It was a microcosm (there's one of those words I'd picked up, again) of society, from the highest to the lowest, and sometimes there wasn't all that much difference between them. In the great scheme of things, the spaces that divide humanity are small.

Dr. Callie Madison and her husband, Jake, were about half a block ahead of us. As I watched, what appeared to be a homeless man came up and started talking to them. Jake shook his head, tightened his hold on Callie's arm, and started moving faster. The man stayed with them, though, and I caught some of what he was saying.

" . . . no place to live since Katrina, man. You can help out a little. . . . All dressed up to go to some fancy party . . ."

Jake Madison stopped short, let go of his wife's arm, and squared up with the panhandler. "I said I don't have anything for you and asked you to leave us alone."

Beside me, Will said, "Uh-oh. You think we should do something about this?"

"I don't know what we can do except look for a cop," I said as I started to do just that. Police officers on foot patrolled the French Quarter, but I didn't see any of them at the moment. That old bit about there never being a cop around when you need one seemed to be coming true right now.

But Will was right. I felt a certain responsibility for the Madisons, since they were my clients. If that panhandler got violent, they might be hurt, and I couldn't just stand by and allow that to happen. I started walking a little faster, my heels clicking rapidly against the sidewalk.

Things happened before Will and I could get there. The

panhandler said in an aggrieved tone, "Hey, man, you don't have to be like that. Remember that 'there but for the grace of God' stuff. You could be me, man."

"Not in a million years," Jake said.

That set the panhandler off. I knew that a lot of them had mental problems or drug addictions and weren't too stable to begin with, and this one certainly wasn't. He started cursing and swung a punch at Jake's head.

But Jake was too fast for him. He ducked under the blow with what seemed like a casual move, and then as he straightened he drove a fist into the panhandler's midsection. It was a short, sharp punch that sent the man stumbling backward. He came up against a lamp post, banged his head on it, and then slid down along the post so that he wound up sitting with his back against it, gasping for air. Jake pointed a blunt finger at him and said, "If you know what's good for you, you'll stay right there, boozy."

Will and I hurried up to the Madisons, and I asked, "Are you folks all right?"

Jake grunted. "I'm fine," he said as if he didn't think he'd been in any danger at all. He turned to his wife. "How about you, Callie?"

"I'm fine, too," she said, but her voice was tight with anger. She glared at her husband and went on, "Did you have to hit him?"

"Hey, he tried to hit me!"

"Would it have killed you to give him a few dollars so he would have just gone on his way?"

"Yeah, he would have gone on his way," Jake said, "and he would have started bothering somebody else. Don't go thinking he would've used any money I gave him for food or a place to stay, though. He would have drunk it up, just like he drinks up all the rest of the money he begs from suckers like you, Callie."

I was sort of agreeing with him until he took that shot at his wife. I thought that wasn't called for.

Callie didn't like it, either. She said, "I may be what you call a sucker, Jake, but at least I have some compassion in my heart."

"Yeah. Just not any passion."

With that wide jaw of hers set tight, she blew out her breath between clenched teeth and shook her head. "Not . . . here," she said.

Jake spread his hands. "Fine. Let's go on to this party. At least they'll have drinks and maybe something to eat, right?"

Callie didn't say anything. She just turned and started stalking along the sidewalk, away from the scene of the brief but violent confrontation.

Jake glanced at Will and shrugged as if to say, "Women, huh?" When he didn't get any response from Will, he turned and went after his wife.

"Funny, I didn't realize we'd gone back in time fifty years," Will said quietly when the Madisons were out of earshot.

"You mean because of the way Jake treats his wife?"

"Yeah. He was pretty rude."

Before I could agree with Will, the panhandler whined, "Hey, I'm the one who got knocked down here! Doesn't anybody feel sorry for me?"

"Quit while you're ahead, pal," I told him. "That guy could've broken you in half."

Will took a five dollar bill out of his pocket and handed it to the man. "Sober up and get something to eat."

"Sure thing, Chief. I'll sure do that."

As Will and I resumed walking, I said, "You know Jake was

39

right about one thing. That guy will just go drink up that money."

"I know," Will said with a sigh. "I can't help it. When I see somebody who's down on their luck, even when it's their own fault, I want to help."

It was debatable whether giving the panhandler money actually helped him or not, but it was also a debate I didn't want to have right now. I was more interested in getting to the reception, and then to the opening ceremony of the festival, and then to that late supper with Will.

We turned the corner. The theater was on the next block, on the right. People were streaming into the impressive red brick building. I spotted Drs. Paige and Jeffords, who seemed to always be together. I wondered for a second if Dr. Paige had taken up with Dr. Jeffords after breaking up with Michael Frasier, but that seemed unlikely to me. For one thing, he was a good thirty years older than her and, for another, he looked like somebody's kindly old grandfather or a popcorn pitchman, take your pick.

The reception was being held in the theater lobby. As Will and I went in, I saw Lawrence Powers talking to a couple of women I recognized from the movie screen. As far as I knew, they hadn't been in any movies based on Tennessee Williams's plays, but they might have performed in them on stage. His son and daughter-in-law stood nearby. June looked like she wished Papa Larry would introduce her to the movie stars while Edgar wore the distracted, slightly bored look that engineers often display when they are out of their element. But, to be fair, a playwright would probably have the exact same expression if he found himself in a roomful of engineers.

A cash bar was set up on one side of the lobby where the harder stuff could be purchased, while waiters circulated through the crowd with trays bearing glasses of complimentary champagne. There was also a long table with cheese, crackers, and other finger food. I was hungry and thought about nibbling a little, but I was willing to wait until Will and I had supper.

The lobby was already crowded and full of talk and laughter. We wandered past the two professors who had done the bulk of the arguing at the airport in Atlanta and during the flight. One of them was saying, "How can you defend the editorial acumen of Farnsworth Wright? He rejected story after story that Lovecraft submitted to him!"

"Yes, but he published 'The Vengeance of Nitocris,' " the other one insisted. "That was Williams's foot in the door."

The first one snorted. "Some foot! It was just a lurid story by a high school kid that made no lasting impression at all. Williams might as well not have sold it to *Weird Tales*."

"It was his first work in print. Wright saw something there."

"Then why didn't he buy anything else from Williams?"

"Thank God he didn't! If that had happened, Willliams might be just another forgotten pulp writer today!"

"So you praise Wright on one hand and damn him on the other, all because of a story that has absolutely no place of importance in the rest of Williams's oeuvre?"

"There always has to be a first story and, anyway, the prevalent themes are already there, right from the start."

Will had paused to listen to the exchange and, as I watched him, I said, "You're just itchin' to get right in the middle of that, aren't you?"

"No, I'm fine," he said. "I think both of their positions are extreme and that the truth lies somewhere in between. As S. T. Joshi has commented about Farnsworth Wright—"

I held up a hand to stop him. "I don't know who any of those folks are, darlin', so why don't you just get us some champagne?"

I was afraid for a second that I'd insulted him, but then he laughed and said, "You're right. Do you want something to eat, too?"

Giving in to temptation, I said, "If they've got some of those little squares of cheese and some crackers, I wouldn't mind that. I'm feelin' a mite peckish, and it'll be a good while yet before we have supper."

Will nodded. "I'll be right back."

He moved off through the crowd, weaving in and out of the available spaces, while I looked around. I saw several tuxedo-clad men and women in evening gowns near the entrance to the theater's auditorium and figured they were the members of the committee that oversaw the festival. I was about to go over and say something to them when a big shape got in front of me.

"Excuse me," Dr. Ian Keller said. "I didn't mean to get in your way."

"That's all right. I'm Delilah Dickinson, by the way."

He smiled. "Sure. Will Burke's friend who arranged the trip for us. I'm grateful to you, Ms. Dickinson. I'm not much of a guy for details. I liked being able to just show up at the airport and go."

He seemed friendly enough, so I thought I could risk a personal question. "You're not from the South, are you?"

That brought a chuckle from him. "Nah, I'm one of those Yankees. Born and raised in New Jersey."

"How'd you wind up bein' an expert on Southern literature? If you don't mind me askin', that is?"

"Not at all," he assured me. "Something about it just . . . resonates with me, I guess you could say. I like the gentler pace not only of Southern literature, but of Southern life as well. I never fit in up north. Too much of a rat race."

"I know the feelin'," I told him. "Unfortunately, Atlanta's gettin' to be the same way."

He nodded. "Yes, I know. But I'd still rather be there than in Newark, no offense to the friends and family I still have up there."

"You still have family there?"

"Well, yeah. A brother. That's all."

I liked Ian Keller. He was a little intimidating because of his size, and he was a Yankee, true enough, but compared to most of the rest of the professors, he was a plain-spoken fella and down to earth. Not like—

Before I could finish that thought, I heard an angry voice shouting, "Where is he? What have you done with him, you bitch? You've stolen my old man!"

CHAPTER 5

I recognized Michael Frasier's voice, and it didn't take much deductive power to figure out that the "bitch" he was yelling at was probably Tamara Paige. I couldn't see them as I looked across the crowded theater lobby, but as a surprised silence fell over the place, I heard Paige respond, "What the hell are you talking about? Get away from me, you lunatic!"

"Not until you tell me what you did with Howard Burleson!" Frasier shouted back.

"Oh, no," I muttered. "Those two are gonna ruin the evening." I started trying to push my way through the crowd, hoping that if I could reach them, I could calm things down and maybe salvage the rest of the reception.

Dr. Keller caught up with me and moved past me. "Let me give you a hand," he said.

He was about six-three and probably weighed two hundred and fifty pounds, which meant that people were a lot more likely to get out of his way than they were to move aside for me. So I got right behind him and let him plow a path through the crowd for me.

By the time we reached Drs. Paige and Frasier, a circle had cleared around them as people backed off from the angry confrontation. The two of them were still yelling at each other.

Frasier wasn't dressed for the reception. He wore slacks and a casual shirt with no jacket or tie, which told me he had intended to stay at the hotel this evening. Something had caused him to come here to the theater, however, and it was obvious that something was the disappearance of Howard Burleson.

I wondered what had happened to the old man and immediately thought that he might have forgotten where he was and wandered off. He could be shuffling around the streets of the French Quarter and getting into all sorts of trouble.

But while that possibility worried the heck out of me, I had more pressing concerns, like keeping Drs. Paige and Frasier from trying to punch each other. Dr. Jeffords was plucking ineffectually at the sleeve of Tamara Paige's dress, but she ignored him as she glared defiantly at Frasier.

"I tell you, I don't have the slightest idea what you're talking about," she insisted. "I haven't seen that old scoundrel you dragged along and persuaded to lie for you, since we got here."

"Who else would have taken him?" Frasier shot back. "And he's not lying!"

"Why would I want to kidnap some delusional geriatric fraud?"

"You're worried that what he'll say during my presentation will invalidate everything you've ever written about Tennessee Williams and *Cat on a Hot Tin Roof*!"

"You're insane!" Dr. Paige spread her arms and then gestured at her body, which was covered by a rather formfitting green dress. "Anyway, do I look like I've got an old man hidden somewhere on me?"

Frasier made a curt, angry slash with his hand in the air. "You've probably got him stashed in your room at the hotel. Or maybe you got him out of there completely and hid him in

46

another hotel. You just want to ruin my presentation tomorrow."

"You're wrong," Dr. Paige said. "I'd much rather you get up there and make a fool of yourself, Michael, so that everyone can see for themselves what I found out a long time ago: as a scholar, you're a complete failure." She sniffed contemptuously. "Just like you're a failure as a man."

That was one too many cheap shots for Frasier to withstand. He took a quick step toward her, his hands coming up as if he wanted to wrap them around her throat and choke the life out of her.

Ian Keller glanced at me and then stepped between them. He was too big for Frasier to get around. "Hold on there, Michael," Keller said in a mild but firm voice. "I think you've made enough of a scene here tonight."

"Get out of my way, Ian," Frasier snapped. "I don't want to hurt you."

The likelihood of Frasier being able to hurt Dr. Keller was so farfetched it made me want to laugh, but I wasn't in a laughing mood at the moment. I was mad and worried at the same time. I stepped up and said, "Dr. Frasier, do you claim that Mr. Burleson has disappeared from the hotel?"

Frasier gave me an impatient glance. "Of course he's disappeared. Would I be here trying to find out what that harpy did with him if he hadn't?"

"Calling folks names isn't going to do anybody any good," I said. "Did you have Mr. Burleson paged at the hotel? It's a big place. Maybe he just got turned around and couldn't find his way back to his room."

"I looked everywhere before I came over here. He's not there." Frasier sent another glare toward Tamara Paige. "She did something with him."

"I most certainly did not!" she said.

Dr. Jeffords cleared his throat and spoke up. "Dr. Paige has been with me most of the time since we arrived, Dr. Frasier. I doubt if she would have had time to abscond with your . . . your companion."

"Don't call him that," Frasier snapped. "He's part of my presentation, that's all."

Dr. Paige said, "You should be more worried that the crazy old coot wandered off somewhere."

That same thought had occurred to me, of course, although without the "crazy old coot" part. I said, "I really think we should alert the authorities that he's missing. If he's wandering around New Orleans alone, he could get hurt."

Will had made his way over from the table with the food. He came up holding a saucer with some squares of cheese and a dozen or so crackers on it. Obviously, he had heard enough of the conversation while he was making his way through the crowd that he knew what was going on, because he said, "I agree. Someone should call the police."

Frasier lifted his hands and said, "Hold on, hold on. Let's not overreact."

That brought a hoot of derisive laughter from Tamara Paige. "Says the man who charged in here accusing me of kidnapping! I ought to sue you for slander."

"It's not slander if it's true," Frasier shot back, his upper lip curling. "And you still haven't proven that it's not."

"I don't have to."

"You do to win a lawsuit for slander."

I said, "You're gettin' off the track again, folks. We need to find Mr. Burleson." I didn't want something else to go wrong with one of my tours. I don't mean an occasional glitch; there are always plenty of those. I was worried about a major snafu, like having a client vanish. And, of course, I was concerned

about Mr. Burleson's welfare, too. I'm not completely merce-
nary.

"He's an old man," I went on. "How long ago did you notice he was missing, Doctor?"

Frasier frowned. "About half an hour ago, I guess."

That would have been about the same time Will and I had
left the St. Emilion to walk over here to the theater. I didn't
recall seeing Burleson in the hotel lobby as we left.

"How long before that was it you saw him last?"

Frasier thought about it for a second, then said, "Maybe another half-hour. I got him settled in his room after we got here,
and then he took a nap. Old people have to have naps."

I wasn't sure I appreciated that comment, since I'd taken a
nap myself before getting ready for the reception, but I let it
go and asked, "What about after that?"

"I went to his room about six to see that he got something
to eat. I called room service and placed the order for him."

"But you didn't stay there until the food came?"

He shook his head. "No. I thought he could handle opening
a door and letting the waiter bring the food in, for God's
sake!" Frasier ran his fingers through his hair in exasperation.
"Obviously, I was wrong."

"Did you check with room service?" Will asked. "Did they
deliver the food?"

"That's the first thing I thought of. They said nobody answered when the waiter knocked at six fifteen."

So whatever had happened to Howard Burleson, it had happened during that fifteen minutes or so after Frasier called
room service. Which meant that by now Burleson had been
gone for about an hour, maybe a little longer.

That was long enough for plenty of things to have happened, and most of them weren't good.

One of the men wearing tuxedos had come over to see what all the commotion was about. He said, "Do I understand that one of the festival's guests is missing?"

"He's not a guest," Frasier said. "He's part of my presentation."

"But he's still a human being," the man said. "I hate to generate any bad publicity for the festival, but I'm calling the police—"

"Wait!" Frasier said. "I don't think that's necessary yet."

He had reacted like that when Will suggested calling the cops a few minutes earlier. I didn't know why Frasier was so opposed to the idea, but clearly he was. Just as clearly, we couldn't afford to stand around talking much longer when an old man's life might be in danger. We might have waited too long already.

"I'm going back to the hotel to have another look around," Frasier went on. "Then if I can't find him, I . . . I'll call the police, I swear."

"I'll come with you," I said. I hated to miss the rest of the reception and the readings afterward, not to mention this mess was threatening the late, intimate supper I had planned with Will. But Howard Burleson was one of my clients, even if I hadn't met him or even heard of him until today, and if he was in trouble, I had a responsibility to help him.

"I'm coming, too," Tamara Paige stated. "I know you're still suspicious of me, Michael, and I want to prove I didn't have anything to do with the old man going missing."

"Fine," Frasier snapped. "Let's just go find him."

I turned to Will. "I'll be back later if I can—"

"I'm coming with you," he broke in as he handed the cheese and crackers to one of the men standing there. "I'm not going to let you wander around the French Quarter alone at night."

"I won't be alone. Dr. Frasier and Dr. Paige are going, too."

"Well, there'll be four of us, then," Will insisted.

I didn't want to waste any more time arguing about that, so I said, "All right, come on. Let's go."

The tuxedo-clad man protested. "I still think we should call the police now."

"Let 'em take a look," Dr. Keller urged. "It won't take long to check and see if the old guy showed up at the hotel since Dr. Frasier left."

That's what I thought. There wouldn't be any leisurely stroll along the sidewalks of the French Quarter this time. I wanted to get back to the St. Emilion as fast as we could.

We left the theater and headed for the hotel, walking fast. I asked Frasier, "Did you actually tell anybody at the hotel that Mr. Burleson is missing?"

He shook his head. "No. The room service operator probably wondered why I was asking if his food had been delivered, but I didn't specifically say that I couldn't find him."

That meant the hotel management wouldn't have notified the authorities, either.

"Does he have Alzheimer's?"

"What?" Frasier snapped in reply to my question. "Howard, you mean?"

"Yeah. Has he been diagnosed with Alzheimer's? Is he on medication for it or for anything else?"

"Not that I know of. His memory's a little fuzzy sometimes, but mostly he's as sharp as he can be."

Dr. Paige said, "Except when he starts trying to convince people that he and Tennessee Williams were lovers."

"They—" Frasier began angrily, then stopped short in his argument. He turned back to me and said, "Why do you want to know if he has Alzheimer's?"

"Because if he doesn't, the police might not even start to

look for him for twenty-four or forty-eight hours, depending on what their policy is here. They'll make an exception, though, if the missing person is delusional or on medication."

"I don't know what medication he's taking," Frasier said. "He never mentioned anything about being delusional, though."

That was just the thing, I thought: if you're delusional, you probably don't know it. You think you're all right and it's the rest of the world that's crazy.

I was also shocked that Frasier would bring a man in his eighties on a trip like this without even knowing what medications he was taking. What if Mr. Burleson had had a medical emergency of some sort? Maybe he carried all that information on him, but maybe he didn't.

That confirmed my hunch that Frasier didn't really care about the old man as a person. Burleson was just a prop for his presentation. A vital prop, maybe, but still a prop.

I saw the hotel ahead of us. I'd been looking at everybody we passed and trying to peer into the windows of every building, too, hoping to spot Howard Burleson. So far, though, there had been no sign of him.

As we reached the hotel, I suggested, "We should talk to that fella Gillette, the assistant manager, if we can find him. I bet he'd be glad to help—and keep quiet about it. He won't want any bad publicity for the hotel."

Will said, "That's a good idea, but he'll probably be even more worried about the hotel's liability in a potential lawsuit."

"I don't care what gets him movin', as long as he helps us find the old man."

When we asked at the concierge's desk for the assistant manager's office, the pretty blond woman on duty there pointed us down a narrow hallway.

"Is there a problem?" she asked with a look of professional concern. "I'd be glad to help if I can."

I shook my head. "We just need to talk to Mr. Gillette for a minute. Is he still there?"

The woman smiled slightly. "Dale's always in his office. I swear, I don't know when he sleeps."

We went down the hallway, and Will knocked on the door. From inside, Gillette called, "Come in."

Will opened the door. Gillette glanced up from his desk, then looked again as he saw all four of us marching in. He came to his feet quickly.

He asked the same question that the concierge had. "Is there a problem?"

"One of your guests has disappeared," Frasier said.

Gillette came out from behind the desk. He looked as dapper and cool as ever, but I saw alarm lurking in his eyes. "Let's all stay calm now," he said. "Who's missing?"

"Howard Burleson."

"The elderly gentleman who was with you when I checked you in this afternoon?"

"That's right."

I saw the relief that appeared on Gillette's face. "Mr. Burleson's not missing," he said. "He's just gone around the corner to Petit Claude's."

All of us stiffened with surprise. "Where?" Frasier demanded.

"It's a jazz club, just around the corner."

"How do you know this?" Will asked.

"Because I ran into Mr. Burleson in the lobby a little while ago, and he asked me if the club was still there. I told him it was and asked him if he was familiar with it. He said that he had been there many times, years ago, with a friend of his."

I had a hunch that the friend Burleson meant was Tennessee Williams, but that didn't matter now.

"He said he was going to take a look at the place again," Gillette continued. "I assume he's still there."

I said, "But you don't know that."

Gillette frowned. "Well, no, I suppose I can't be sure he's there. You could check his room—"

"He's not there," Frasier said as he started to turn toward the door. "Where exactly is this club? I have to find him!"

"I'll show you," Gillette offered. His manner was brisk as he led us out of his office. I suppose he had realized that Burleson could have wandered off anywhere after visiting Petit Claude's, and now he was worried again. He said, "You know, if Mr. Burleson is, well, mentally disadvantaged, someone should be with him at all times. I must say, though, he struck me as being fine. He seemed to know exactly where he was and what he was doing."

"Of course he did," Frasier said, with a glance at Tamara Paige. "There's nothing wrong with his memory."

Even under these strained circumstances, he couldn't let go of the hostility between him and Dr. Paige, and, judging by her glare, neither could she.

The five of us left the hotel, turning in the other direction from the way Will and I had gone to the theater. It was noisier on the street now, as the evening's hilarity began to increase. Along with the humidity and the smells of Cajun cooking, the air was full of loud talk, laughter, and music from various outdoor restaurants and clubs. Most of it was Dixieland jazz or blues, but I heard a little zydeco mixed in, too. It made for a discordant but somehow pleasing blend.

When we turned the corner, I saw the neon sign for Petit Claude's. It was a little place, not much more than a hole-in-the-wall that was crowded between a sports bar and a bakery that was closed for the night. The place had an air of age about it. Maybe it was the way the sign buzzed and flickered from time to time, or maybe it was the patina of softness that the years had worn onto the bricks of the building's façade. A green awning extended over the sidewalk at the entrance, and it looked like it had been there since the Truman administration. Maybe even since FDR.

"There it is," Gillette said. "I'm sure he's in there."

"He had better be," Frasier said, not bothering to keep the anger and menace out of his voice. "From now on, he's not to leave the hotel without me."

"I'm afraid we can't be held responsible for enforcing something like that, Dr. Frasier. That's up to you."

"You can spread the word among your people that he shouldn't be wandering around by himself, can't you?"

Gillette shrugged. "I suppose I can do that."

We had reached the club. A black doorman who also looked like he'd been there since the Truman administration gave us a toothless grin and said, "How you folks doin' this fine night? Come to listen to some good hot jazz, have you?"

"Have you seen an old man?" Frasier asked sharply.

"Besides in the mirror, you mean? I've seen lots o' elderly gentlemen come an' go through this here door, sir. Just 'cause a man gettin' on up in years don't mean he stops lovin' that hot music."

"Oh, just step aside," Frasier snapped. He caught hold of the door's handle and pulled it open, jerking it out of the old man's hand.

"Hey!" Gillette said, beating me to it. "There's no need to act like that."

Frasier wasn't listening, though. He stalked into the club with the rest of us trailing behind him. As I passed the doorman, I said, "Sorry."

"Don't you worry your head 'bout it, miss," he said. "One thing ain't never been in short supply in the Quarter is jack-asses." He grinned. "They used to pull wagons 'long these very streets. Now they go inside."

I couldn't help but grin back at him. Then I followed the others into the club.

Packed into its narrow, dimly lit confines were a bar along the left-hand wall, shadowy booths on the right-hand wall, and a few tables in between. At the back of the room was a postage-stamp-size bandstand where a man was playing a trumpet, backed up by a piano and bass in a classic trio. The music was hot, all right, fast and sweaty, the sort where the notes reached right inside your guts and jangled them all around. Just listening to it made your feet want to move.

Or in the case of Howard Burleson, instead of tapping his feet, he patted the table as he sat in one of the booths. There was a glass of clear liquid in front of him, but I would have bet it wasn't water. His hat sat on the table beside the glass. His bald head gleamed, even in this place, where there wasn't much light.

"Thank God!" Frasier exclaimed, loud enough so that some of the club's patrons turned to glance at him disapprovingly. The place was almost but not quite full.

"He's still here," Gillette said, sounding very relieved. "If you don't need me anymore, I'll get back to the hotel."

Frasier ignored him and headed for the booth where Burleson sat. Gillette nodded to the rest of us and went back out the door.

A waitress started to ask Frasier if he wanted a drink, but he waved her away. The rest of us followed him over to the booth where Burleson sat. Along the way, Will caught the waitress's eye, made a little motion with his hand, and shook his head.

As Frasier came to a stop beside the booth, he said, "Howard, what are you doing here?"

Burleson evidently hadn't noticed us until now. He looked up with a dreamy smile on his weathered face and said, "There you are, Michael. I came to listen to some music. You and your friends should sit down. Those boys are really good."

"We don't have time for music," Frasier said. "We need to get back to the hotel. Come on, Howard."

Burleson kept patting the table softly in time with the music. "Not just yet, not just yet. I'm havin' a good time. So many memories in this place. So many wonderful memories. Tom and I used to come here, you know."

I glanced at Tamara Paige, thinking that she might make some disparaging comment, but for once she kept her mouth shut about the subject of Howard Burleson and Tennessee Williams. Maybe she felt a little sorry for the old man. Her face seemed a little softer than it had been earlier.

Frasier insisted, "You can tell everybody all about that tomorrow, Howard. Right now, we need to go back to the hotel." He reached out and closed his hand around Burleson's skinny arm. "Come on." It was an order now, issued in a hard, angry voice.

"Take it easy, Michael," Tamara said. "Mr. Burleson wants to listen to some music. I don't see any harm in it, especially when it's as good as that song they're playing now."

Burleson beamed up at her. "You like Dixieland, my dear?"

"Sure," she said with a shrug. "I like all sorts of music."

"So do I, so do I." With his free hand, Burleson waved toward the seat on the other side of the booth. "Why don't you sit down and join me? Why don't all of you?" He lowered his voice a little and added, "Michael, you're hurtin' me."

With what sounded like a muttered curse, Frasier let go of

the old man's arm. In a strangled voice, he said, "All right, we'll all sit down for a little while. But then we have to go back to the hotel, all right, Howard?"

Burleson had started nodding along with the music. "That'll be fine." His skinny body swayed a little from side to side. He smiled at Tamara and said, "You sit down here next to me, honey."

I could tell that Frasier didn't like that idea at all. He would have preferred to keep Dr. Paige as far away from Burleson as he possibly could. But for now, he was trying to play along with the old man in hopes of cajoling him out of there that much sooner. I could see that cold calculation on his face.

Burleson slid over enough for Tamara to sit down beside him. Meanwhile, Will, Frasier, and I crowded into the other side of the booth. I was between the two men and didn't like it. Sitting next to Michael Frasier was sort of like cuddling up with a badger.

"Y'all need somethin' to drink now," Burleson said. He started to raise a hand to signal the waitress, but Frasier shook his head.

"We're fine, Howard. We won't be here very long, remember? We have to get back to the hotel."

"It's a nice hotel," Burleson said. "I remember it, although I don't think I ever stayed there before. I had a place on the Vieux Carré, a little apartment where Tom sometimes visited me. Mostly, though, we came here to listen to the music and sip on cordials. It was a wonderful time, just wonderful. The light had more colors in it then, and when the breeze blew, it was like warm fingers caressin' your face. If only things could have stayed like that, instead of the years ravagin' us all with those horrible appetites of theirs. If only time wouldn't rip those moments of happiness away from us like it was jealous and couldn't stand to see us that way . . ."

Despite his age, Howard Burleson still had a warm, rich voice, and when he started talking that way, I enjoyed listening to him. Maybe he really had known Tennessee Williams. The reminiscences reminded me of the voice that permeated Williams's plays.

"It was right here," Burleson went on. "Right here at this very table." He patted its scarred surface again, not keeping time with the music now but more of a tender gesture, like a man touching the head of an old and beloved pet.

"What was right here, Mr. Burleson?" I asked.

Before he could answer, Frasier leaned forward and practically snarled, "Not one word, Howard, you hear me? Not . . . one . . . word."

"Let the man talk," Tamara said with a quick frown at Frasier. Then she turned to the old man and went on, "What was it, Mr. Burleson? What happened here?"

Frasier made a strangled sound, and for a second I thought he was going to leap across the booth and clap a hand over Burleson's mouth. That was the only way he could have stopped the words that came from Burleson's lips.

But he held himself in check, and Howard Burleson said, "Why, it was right here at this very table, darlin', that I wrote *Cat on a Hot Tin Roof.*"

CHAPTER 6

That statement flabbergasted three of us at the table. Frasier was the only one who wasn't surprised. He put his elbows on the table, dropped his head into his hands, and let out a low groan. Without looking up, he said, "Howard . . . Howard, I told you not to say anything about that until the presentation."

"I can understand why," Tamara said. "That's insane!"

For the first time, Burleson looked offended. "You're just as charmin' as you can be, my dear, but really, you shouldn't impugn a creator's integrity. My authorship of that play means a great deal to me, and I intend to set the record straight."

Tamara managed to smile as she looked at him and said, "I'm sorry, Mr. Burleson. I didn't mean to offend you, honestly I didn't. But the authorship of Tennessee Williams's plays has never been in any doubt. It's not like, say, Shakespeare, where we don't really know who wrote them—"

"I wrote *Cat on a Hot Tin Roof,* I tell you." Burleson was starting to look and sound a little angry now. "It was an autobiographical play."

"Well, yes, in that Big Daddy Pollitt is clearly based on Williams's own father, C. C. Williams—"

Burleson broke in again. "No, you don't understand. I'm Brick." He tapped himself on his thin chest. "I'm Brick."

He looked about as unlike Paul Newman as he possibly could, I thought, but he seemed absolutely sincere.

"That's . . . not possible," Tamara said slowly. "Brick comes from a short story Williams wrote called 'Three Players of a Summer Game.' It's very well known among Williams scholars."

Burleson nodded as if she had just proved his point. "He was strugglin' with that story when I met him in Venice. Brick wasn't even in the first draft. He put Brick in there after I told him about my daddy and my . . . my wife. And then when we got back here to New Orleans, he said that there wasn't a play in the story after all. That's how he did it most of the time, you know. He'd write a story first, to get everything straight in his head about what he wanted to say, and then he would turn it into a play."

"I know," Tamara said with a nod. "I've read all the short stories."

"So have I." Burleson sniffed a little. "The plays are better, but then, they were supposed to be. Tom never cared that much about the stories. Writin' them was just a tool he used to figure things out."

"But you're saying he didn't base *Cat on a Hot Tin Roof* on 'Three Players of a Summer Game'? Because it's obvious that he did, even though there are a number of differences."

"No, ma'am," Burleson said with an adamant shake of his head. "The play is so much different than the story because I wrote it after Tom decided not to, basin' it on my own family and my life."

Frasier slapped his hands against his temples and said, "Why don't you just tell them everything, you . . . you . . ." He couldn't finish.

"All right, I will," Burleson said. He tapped the table this time, harder, with one fingertip. "I sat right here at this very table and wrote that play with my own hand. You see, even though I hadn't known Tom for very long, I had learned a great deal from him in that time. And I'd always been a follower of his work, even before I knew him. He was quite a favorite of mine."

Will leaned forward, clasped his hands together on the table, and asked, "Did you give the manuscript to him to read?"

"Dr. Burke!" Tamara said. "Don't tell me you're taking this seriously?"

"I'd like to hear whatever Mr. Burleson has to say," Will replied, and at that moment I liked him more than I ever had before, which was considerable. He smiled, nodded across the table at the old man, and said, "Go on, Mr. Burleson."

"Well, of course I gave it to him to read," Burleson said. "I valued his opinion. After all, he was a highly respected dramatist by that time. He'd already had two big hits on Broadway and in the movies, *The Glass Menagerie* and *A Streetcar Named Desire*. I thought he could tell me if it was any good or not."

Burleson stroked his fingertips across the table, as if he were searching for memories in the grain of the wood.

"We sat here in this booth while Tom read the pages. I think at first he was doing it just to be kind, you know, because he didn't want to offend me. And if he had told me that it was bad, I would have believed him. If he had told me I should go and burn it or throw it in the river, I probably would have.

"But I saw him start to sit up straighter, and his fingers tightened on the pages so that they crinkled a little, and he forgot to take a drink. He laid the pages aside one by one as he finished them, and at first they were in a neat stack, with all the edges squared. But then his hand began to shake and so when the pages began to pile up, they weren't exactly straight anymore. The edges were . . . ragged. I knew then that what he was reading was making an impression on him. He was surprised, surprised that what I had written was actually good."

He had me in his spell by this time, and judging by the looks on the faces of Will and Tamara, they felt the same way. When Burleson paused to take a small sip from his glass of liquor, the three of us leaned forward slightly in anticipation. We wanted him to go on. We wanted to know what had happened next.

Michael Frasier still looked angry and despairing. He had heard all this before.

But the rest of us hadn't, and there was almost a sigh of relief around the table as Burleson licked his lips and then went on. "When Tom was finished, he didn't say anything. That was unusual, you know. He was a great talker most of the time. I could sit and listen to that man talk for hours, and the things he said were as good or better than what he wrote down in his plays. That's why he had so many good friends over the years. One reason, anyway.

"But to get back to what I was sayin' . . . Tom just sat there and looked at me for a minute or two, and then he said, 'Howard'—that's what he called me, Howard, never Howie or anything like that—he said, 'Howard, there's somethin' here.' And he reached over and touched the pages. 'There's somethin' here,' he said to me, 'and it's good.'

"Well, as you might expect, I was very pleased by that reaction. I had thought that he might tell me that it was . . . interestin' . . . or unique . . . or one of those other things you say when somebody you care about has shown you somethin' they've done and you don't want to hurt their feelin's but it's not really good. Like when you look at an ugly baby and say, 'My, he's some boy, ain't he?' You know what I mean?"

Around the table, three heads nodded.

"But Tom didn't say that. He said it was good. But then . . . then he said, 'It needs some work, though.' "

Burleson leaned back against the booth's Naugahyde seat and spread his bony hands.

"That didn't surprise me, mind you. I didn't think that I was so talented I could write somethin' like that for the first time in my life and have it be perfect. But to have Tom say it was good . . . to have Tennessee Williams himself say that my play was good . . . well, that's all I could really think about just then. I figured he could tell me what needed to be fixed and maybe even suggest some things I could do to improve it, but then he said, 'I'll take it and work on it.'

"I tell you what, for a minute that didn't even get through to my brain, I was so happy. But then it did, and I told him I never meant for him to have to take on a chore like that. I knew he was a busy man, always writin', writin' like it was air and water to him, and he had to deal with those producers and directors all the time, in New York and Hollywood, and I told him I didn't want him to bother his head with a piddlin' little thing like my play.

" 'I insist,' he said. 'It's good, but it needs a professional hand now and, after all . . . it is based on my short story.'

"Well, there was no disputin' the truth of that. I'd taken some of what he wrote in that story and used it in the play, but only a little, a very little. Most of it came right from my own life. I had never told him that I came from a well-to-do family, although he might have figured that out from the way I was travelin' 'round Europe when he met me, and I'd never said anything about how I was married once, before I realized that I just . . . wasn't cut out to be married. So he didn't know, right there at first, that all of that was me. That those words had my heart and my soul in 'em. I guess he thought that I had . . .

made it all up. I don't think he saw, really saw, what it meant to me.

"But . . . he was Tennessee Williams. I guess he thought I'd be flattered, and I was, I truly was. And I didn't want to offend him, so I said that if he really thought the play was good and he was really interested in workin' on it, I supposed that would be all right. We would work on it together. Whip it into shape, he said. And then we'd give it to his agent and she would arrange to have it produced on Broadway, and then Hollywood would come a-knockin' and they would make a movie out of it . . . but to do that, the play would have to have his name on it, too, of course, he said. 'By Tennessee Williams and Howard Burleson,' he said. That's what the play would say. But when the time came for all those wonderful, wonderful things to happen—and they did happen—that's not what it said. It said *Cat on a Hot Tin Roof* by Tennessee Williams, and nobody ever knew about Howard Burleson. By then Tom was in New York, and he wouldn't take my calls, and I don't know what he done with all my letters . . . burned 'em, more'n likely . . . and I never saw him or talked to him again."

The old man had been talking for a long time. His voice was cracked and hoarse as he finished his story. He picked up his glass again and sipped the liquor. A long, soft sigh came out of him. Silence hung over the table. The trio on the bandstand had stopped playing sometime while Burleson was talking, and I hadn't noticed. I doubted if Will or Tamara had, either.

Finally, Tamara said, "That's a very touching story, Mr. Burleson. Almost tragic. But how come no one has ever heard of it before? Something as big and important as Tennessee Williams taking credit for a play he didn't write . . . don't you think rumors of it would have surfaced before now?"

"How could they?" Burleson asked. "Tom and I were the

only ones who knew about it, and once I realized what was happenin', I was so devastated I tried to put the whole thing outta my mind. I went back to Atlanta—that's where my family is from, you know—and tried to forget all about Tom Williams and the play and that whole time in my life. I've lived there quietly ever since. I had a small inheritance to support me, you know, and my needs are few. I have books and music and a few friends. A man can live with that and nothing more if he puts his mind to it. I would have gone on like that, if not for that devil, time. My granddaughter—"

"You have a granddaughter?" Tamara interrupted. "But I thought you were . . . I mean . . ."

"Not the type to have offspring?" Burleson asked with a smile. "Ah, but I told you, there was a time when I was married. In those days, people like me didn't live as openly as they do now. And in truth, I think I was trying to deny my true nature. But yes, I had a wife, and I had two children, and in due time, I had grandchildren as well. Great-grandchildren by now, I'm sure, maybe even great-great-grandchildren." He shook his head slowly. "I have never been close to my family since returning from Europe. Their choice, not mine. Except for Natalie, the granddaughter I spoke of. She has taken it upon herself to look after her dear old homosexual granddad. Last year, after I fell and nearly broke my hip, she insisted that I come to live with her. She was very persistent."

I was glad to hear that he had somebody looking out for him, at least. Somebody besides Dr. Michael Frasier. Somebody who actually cared about him.

Will asked, "How did Dr. Frasier find out about your story?"

Frasier sighed. "You have to know everything, don't you? Nobody's willing to leave me anything for my presentation tomorrow." Bitterly, he went on, "Go ahead and tell them, Howard. Tell them the whole thing."

Livia J. Washburn

"There's no need to be like that, Michael," Burleson said. "These nice folks asked. It wouldn't be polite for me not to tell 'em what they want to know."

Frasier scooted toward me, bumping his hip against mine in a mighty unwelcome manner. "Let me out," he snapped. "I need a drink, and I don't need to hear all this again."

Will and I got up so that Frasier could slide out of the booth. He went across the dim, narrow room to the bar while Will and I sat down again. I have to admit, it was a lot nicer there with Frasier gone.

"You were going to tell us how you got involved with Dr. Frasier," Tamara prompted.

Burleson nodded. "Like everything else, it was fate, I suppose. The universe movin' in an endless dance to music of it's own makin'. You see, I was in a bookstore. I love bookstores, especially the ones with old books. I love to just stand there and take a deep breath and drink in the smells of paper and leather and dust. Even when it makes me sneeze, it's worth it to experience that wonderful smell."

He looked around at us and smiled.

"Ah, but you folks are young. You're growin' impatient with the natterin's of a decrepit old man."

"Not at all," Will said without hesitation. "Please go on, Mr. Burleson. We want to hear the rest of the story."

Tamara and I nodded to make sure Burleson understood.

"Very well. I was in a bookstore"—he named the place, an antiquarian bookstore I had heard of but never visited—"and I was browsin' through the selection when I saw another customer, a young man, lookin' at a copy of *Cat on a Hot Tin Roof*. I don't have any earthly idea what possessed me to do it, but suddenly I was seized with the impulse to speak to him, to tell him what he was really lookin' at, to speak the truth to someone, anyone, after all those years. . . . So I said to him, I said,

68

'Despite what's printed in that book, young man, I wrote that play, you know.' "

"And that was Michael?" Tamara asked.

"Indeed it was," Burleson said. "And I must say, startin' out, he was rather rude to me."

Tamara said, "Huh. I'm not surprised."

"He moved away as if I was botherin' him and didn't say anything. And again, I don't really know what moved me to continue the conversation, but I said, 'You don't believe me.'

"He looked at me then and said, 'Of course I don't believe you. Tennessee Williams wrote *Cat on a Hot Tin Roof*.'

"And I said, 'He put his name on it, but I wrote it.' I started telling him about how Tom and I met in Venice and then came back to New Orleans, and how Tom wrote that little story of his and then abandoned it, and how I picked up the gauntlet and wrote the true story of the Burleson family of Atlanta, Georgia. Only I used the name Tom came up with, Pollitt, and moved the settin' so not everybody would know that I was writin' about my own family. And by the time I'd told him all that, he was interested, mighty interested, whether he wanted to admit it or not. After that, I wound up tellin' him everything. He came to believe me . . ." Burleson smiled. "And here we are, in this wonderful old place. I feel like I've come home at last, like this is where I was truly meant to be." The old man's mouth tightened. "Not in some cookie-cutter house in the suburbs where everybody looks alike and thinks alike. My granddaughter, bless her heart, does not provide an atmosphere that's hospitable to a creative soul such as mine. The only reason I agreed to stay with her was because she said she could have me declared incompetent and place me in some . . . some home for old people."

The sneering emphasis he gave the word "home" made it clear he would consider such a place anything but. I understood what he meant. I wouldn't have wanted to wind up in one of those places, either, unless my health was so bad I didn't have a choice.

"Natalie meant well," Burleson went on. "I'm sure she did. She really does have a kind heart. But sometimes I just have to get out of there and be around my own kind again. And by that I mean . . . literary folks. Book people."

Will said, "That's why you were in the bookstore that day when you ran into Michael."

Burleson nodded. "Exactly. I confess, I snuck out and called a cab." He laughed. "I'm a terrible old man, ain't I?"

"I don't think so," I said. "But something bothers me."

"Well, I wouldn't want so lovely a young woman as you to be bothered, my dear. What is it? Tell me."

"No offense, but it seems strange to me that Dr. Frasier would just believe your story about writing *Cat on a Hot Tin Roof* when you didn't have any proof."

Tamara nodded. "I thought of the same thing. You don't have any real evidence to back up your story, Mr. Burleson."

He smiled at us. "Oh, but I do. I have the manuscript . . . the original, handwritten manuscript of *Cat on a Hot Tin Roof* . . . by Howard Burleson."

CHAPTER 7

For the second time tonight, we were left staring in mingled surprise and disbelief at the old man. Will spoke up first, saying, "You have the original holographic manuscript?"

"That's right. Written in my own hand, on this very table." Burleson ran his fingers over the table again. "I can show you the places where my pen slipped into the scars and irregularities of the wood and it left marks on the paper . . . just like our lives slip into the scars and irregularities of the world and it leaves marks on our hearts."

I thought he was reaching a little with that one, but what do I know?

Tamara said, "That's how you convinced Michael? By showing him the manuscript?"

"Yes, indeed. He was quite fascinated. And when he was through pouring over it, he believed what I had told him. He knew that I was the true author of that wonderful play."

"You're aware that any such manuscript would have to be subjected to extensive textual analysis, not to mention forensic testing to determine the age of the paper and ink, before the academic community could even begin to lend any credence to your claims?"

Burleson nodded. "Dr. Frasier has done so. He is convinced."

"Yes, but he's just one man. To achieve any real acceptance, you're going to have to convince many, many more people. Hundreds, maybe thousands."

"I stand prepared to do so, my dear," Burleson declared.

"You brought the manuscript with you?" Will asked.

Burleson shook his head. "Certainly not. Michael made me understand that it's far too valuable for that. I did, however, bring a few sample pages from the original so that they could be displayed as part of Michael's presentation and then examined by the appropriate people." He smiled at Tamara. "Includin' you, I hope, Dr. Paige. Michael tells me that you've made a special study of *Cat on a Hot Tin Roof* in your career. In fact, he says that everything you've ever done depends on it."

"He does, does he?" Tamara asked tightly. She understood, and so did I, what Frasier really meant by that. By dropping this bombshell at the conference, Frasier hoped to knock the legs out from under everything Tamara had ever written about the play. In light of his discovery, all her work and research would be meaningless.

If Howard Burleson was telling the truth, of course.

"Where are those manuscript pages?" I asked.

"In my bag at the hotel."

"The bag Dr. Frasier wouldn't let that porter carry in?"

"That's right."

I understood now why Frasier had been so protective about that bag. He was actually taking a pretty big gamble here. If he couldn't convince his fellow professors that Burleson was telling the truth, he could easily wind up a laughingstock and ruin his own career instead of Tamara Paige's. For him, everything was riding not only on Burleson but also on those sample pages from the manuscript.

"This has all been fascinating, Mr. Burleson," Tamara said,

"but I think we should get back to the hotel now before it gets too late. You have a big day coming up tomorrow, and you need your rest."

Burleson sighed and nodded. "I am gettin' a mite tired. But it's been so nice spendin' part of the evenin' with you young people."

"Maybe when we get back," Tamara went on, "you could show me those pages . . ."

Burleson began to frown and shake his head. "I don't know. Michael told me not to let anyone look at them until the presentation. . . . Of course, now that I think about it, I believe he told me not to tell anyone about how I wrote the play, either, and I've just done that, now, haven't I?"

Tamara leaned closer to him and said, "I really don't think it would hurt anything—"

"What?" Frasier said suddenly from beside the booth. "You don't think what would hurt anything?"

He had been sitting at the bar nursing a beer while Will, Tamara, and I talked to Burleson—well, listened to the old man more than anything, really. Frasier was risking his career and his reputation.

Burleson looked up at Frasier, ignoring Tamara's attempt to shush him, and said, "This charmin' young woman wants to look at those pages from my play, Michael. I don't think it would hurt anything to show them to her, do you?"

Frasier glared at Tamara and said, "You bitch! What are you trying to do?"

Her eyes blazing with anger, she started to get to her feet. Burleson put a hand on her arm to stop her, though, and said, "Now, Michael, there's no call for language like that. You shouldn't insult Dr. Paige just because she's interested in my play."

"She's not interested in your play, Howard, she's interested in ruining me. She probably wants to destroy those pages so no one can ever study them."

"I most certainly do not," Tamara insisted. "I'm as much of a Williams scholar as you are." She paused, and rolled her eyes, for a second. "More, actually. If there's any chance Mr. Burleson is telling the truth, I want to know about it. I just want to confirm his story."

"Forget it. I've already confirmed it. You'll hear all about it tomorrow, and you'll see all the proof you need. Until then, just leave us the hell alone." Frasier looked at Burleson. "Come on, Howard. I let you talk to these people, even though I shouldn't have. It's time to go back to the hotel now."

"I . . . I didn't mean to cause any trouble," Burleson said, starting to look like a little kid who's been caught getting into mischief. "I just wanted to see this old place again, where I had so many happy times, and listen to the music—"

Frasier got control of his anger with a visible effort. "It's all right, Howard. I'm not mad at you. Just remember who brought you here to New Orleans so you could relive those old times. Remember who's going to make you famous, so that you'll finally get credit for your work."

"I suppose you're right." Burleson gave Tamara a sad smile. "If you'll pardon me, my dear . . ." He looked across the table at Will and me. "And if you two lovely people will excuse me . . . I suppose I should return to the hotel with my friend Michael."

I wanted to tell him that Frasier wasn't his friend, that the professor was just using him.

But what if Burleson really was telling the truth, I suddenly asked myself. What if he really had written that play? Didn't he deserve to finally get some credit for it, as Frasier had said? Maybe Frasier's motives weren't the purest in the world—I was convinced he was doing this in hopes of hurting Tamara Paige's career as much as he was to advance his own—but he was the one who believed what the old man was saying. He was the only one who had demonstrated any faith in Howard Burleson.

Maybe the best thing to do, I realized, was to just let this thing play out.

"You go on with Dr. Frasier," I told Burleson. Then I looked at Frasier and added, "And keep a better eye on him this time, Doctor."

"I will," Frasier said grimly. "You can count on that."

Tamara frowned at me. "You're taking quite a bit of responsibility on yourself, aren't you, Ms. Dickinson?"

"I am responsible," I told her. "I'm the leader of this tour. And I don't see how spendin' the rest of the evening fussin' over all this is going to help anything."

"I'm just trying to get to the bottom of Mr. Burleson's story."

"You'll have a chance to do that tomorrow," I pointed out. "We just got a sneak peak of what the whole conference will hear about soon enough. I imagine you'll have plenty of chances to ask questions of Mr. Burleson and examine those manuscript pages."

"That's right," Frasier said. "Thank you, Ms. Dickinson, for being the voice of reason."

I didn't want Frasier's gratitude. He still struck me as a smarmy little weasel. But Burleson had started to look pretty worn out from all the talking and arguing, and I didn't see any point in putting him through more.

"You professors can hash all this out tomorrow. Mr. Burleson needs to go get some rest, though."

He smiled and said, "I am startin' to feel a mite peaked."

Tamara slid out of the booth so he could get up. "All right,

Mr. Burleson," she said. "I'm going to want to ask you a lot of questions tomorrow, though."

He smiled at her as he slowly climbed out of the booth. "Of course, my dear. I'd be tickled pink to talk to you about whatever you want."

Will and I slid out of the booth, too. As we stood up, Frasier looked at the two of us and Tamara and said, "I suppose it's too much to hope that you'll all keep your mouths shut about this."

"Why should I do you any favors?" Tamara shot back at him. "Ruining your big surprise would be just about what you deserve."

Burleson turned to her and said, "Oh, please don't do that, honey. The boy's worked so hard to impress y'all."

Something made Frasier's jaw tighten with anger, I saw; probably being called "the boy." But he didn't say anything, and after a second, Tamara shrugged.

"All right," she said. "I'll let you go ahead and make a fool of yourself, Michael. I've said all along that I was all right with that."

"I won't say anything, either," Will promised. He smiled. "I'd sort of like to see the reaction when Mr. Burleson gets up and tells his story. It's quite a yarn."

"Thank you, young man," Burleson said with a smile of his own.

Frasier looked at me. "What about you?"

I held up both hands, palms out. "Leave me out of this. I'm not a professor, and I don't care who wrote *Cat on a Hot Tin Roof.*"

They all looked at me then like I was a little crazy, even Burleson. But really, it didn't matter to me. I didn't have any stake in this controversy. All I cared about was keeping things running smoothly and getting everybody back to Atlanta safely.

As far as I was concerned, somebody could claim Tennessee Williams was really an alien from outer space, and it would be just fine.

"All right." Frasier took Burleson's arm, and I was glad to see that he was more careful about it this time. "Come along, Howard."

"Oh," Burleson said, "my hat."

Will picked the hat up and handed it to him. Burleson held it poised over his head for a second before he put it on and nodded to us.

"Good evenin', y'all," he said. "Pleasant dreams."

He shuffled out of Petit Claude's with Frasier at his side. When they were gone, Tamara turned to us and said, "Don't believe all that nonsense. It was a good story, but he's either delusional or he's made the whole thing up on purpose, to try to get some attention. There's no way on earth that old man really wrote *Cat on a Hot Tin Roof.*"

"I'd say that's yet to be determined," Will replied. "I'll admit, I'm pretty skeptical, but I'm willing to give him the benefit of the doubt for now."

Tamara said, "How can you say that? *Cat* is obviously the work of the same author who wrote all the other Tennessee Williams plays. The themes and structure are similar, the rhythm of the language is the same—"

"Mr. Burleson said he was a fan of Williams's work," Will pointed out. "Plus, if he really was romantically involved with Williams, they would have spent a lot of time together. He could have picked up the speech patterns, understood the way Williams thought—"

Tamara cut him off by shaking her head. "I'm sorry. I don't buy it. I just don't buy it."

I said, "I'm sure you academic types will figure it all out." I had looked at my watch and seen that by now the festival's opening ceremonies were over. I thought Will and I could still make it for that late supper reservation, though. I slipped my arm through his and said, "Can you get back to the hotel by yourself, Dr. Paige?"

"Of course. It's right around the corner."

"Then Dr. Burke and I have a previous engagement we need to get to."

"Oh. All right." She nodded to us. "Good night."

She went one way when we left Petit Claude's, and Will and I went the other. "That was an amazing story, wasn't it?" he said as we walked along Bourbon Street.

"Amazing," I agreed. "But sometimes the truth is pretty far-fetched."

"Yes, I've learned that." He grinned. "Especially since meeting you."

I thought about punching him on the arm for that one. But instead I just grinned back at him, and we went on to supper.

We made it to the intimate little bistro a few blocks from the hotel in time for our supper reservation. I had been there before, back when I was married and my husband and I vacationed in New Orleans. The place hadn't changed much, and I realized that it might have been a mistake to come here with Will. Remembering the good time I'd had here with my ex didn't do much for the romantic atmosphere.

I tried to put all that out of my mind and concentrate on the present. The food was as good as ever. Instead of ordering from the menu, I explained to Will, you could just tell the chef, "Feed me," and he would come to the table and tell you what he was going to prepare, which was always delicious. He started us off with gumbo and fried green tomatoes, then followed up with chicken creole and crab and asparagus salad.

The wonderful food, along with the dimly lit elegance and comfort of the café, made me relax after the stressful evening.

Even so, I wasn't quite able to get in the mood I'd hoped to, and Will seemed to sense that. Over brandy after we'd finished the meal, while soft music played from hidden speakers, he said, "It's been a pretty tiring day, Delilah, and the conference starts at nine in the morning. I hope you won't mind if I turn in early tonight."

I smiled at him and said, "I was thinking the same thing myself. Herdin' a bunch of folks around will just wear you out, won't it?"

He grinned. "Especially when some of them hate each other and don't mind making a scene."

"We've had some doozies, haven't we?"

"I expect excitement on one of your tours. I remember—"

I held up a hand to stop him. "Don't start talkin' about what happened on that plantation. I've tried to put all that behind me."

"All right. I understand. Anyway, I never expected anything as potentially mind-boggling as this business about Tennessee Williams to come up."

"Is it really that big a deal?" I asked. "Would it be such a shock if it turned out the old man was tellin' the truth?"

"Well, I suppose in the big scheme of things, the question of who really wrote *Cat on a Hot Tin Roof* doesn't mean much. It doesn't have any effect on people's everyday lives. Such a discovery would definitely cause a stir in university English and drama departments around the world, but not as much as it once would have. Williams is a DWM, after all."

I frowned at him, not knowing what he meant.

"Dead white male," Will elaborated. "English departments in general don't lavish as much attention on authors as they once did. This particular crowd, though, the folks at this festival, it'll be a big deal to them. You can count on that."

"There won't be a riot or anything when Frasier makes his presentation, will there?"

"I don't know," Will said, but then his smile told me that he was just joking.

We left the café a short time after that and headed back to the hotel. We had lingered over supper, so it was fairly late by now, about eleven o'clock. Of course, even at this hour, the streets of the French Quarter were fairly busy. The sidewalks still had plenty of people on them, talking and laughing, and I could still hear music in the air.

I looked around the lobby when we got to the St. Emilion and saw several people I recognized from our group sitting around talking, and I figured there would be more of them in the bar. Will nodded pleasantly to some of the folks we passed, but we didn't stop to talk. We went up in the elevator to the third floor, and when we got to my room, he stepped just inside with me and gave me an old-fashioned good-night kiss that made me reconsider my decision to turn in early. Only for a moment, though. I really was tired and wanted to get some sleep. I planned on being up bright and early the next morning, in case anybody from the group needed help with anything.

He said, "I'll see you in the morning. Good night."

"'Night, Will. It was a nice evenin' . . . after we got past the disappearin' old man and all that."

He chuckled. "Yeah. See you."

I eased the door closed, threw the deadbolt, and put the chain on. Then I sighed and shook my head. Will Burke was probably the nicest fella I knew and I sure enjoyed spending time with him, but I didn't know if I wanted things to get any more serious than they already were. I knew I wouldn't mind getting married again someday, but I wasn't sure I wanted to be a professor's wife.

"Don't go gettin' ahead of yourself, Delilah," I told myself out loud, then turned away from the door and went on into the sumptuous room without turning on any lights. There was enough glow from the windows for me to find my way around.

Something drew me toward the balcony on the other side of the room. I opened the curtains, unfastened the French doors, and stepped out to look around the atrium and down into the garden. Discreetly placed lamps in the trees gave off enough light for folks to find their way around. It was peaceful and beautiful, and once again I was struck by how much it looked like a little piece of jungle right here inside the hotel.

I spotted a man walking along one of the paths and recognized him as Dr. Ian Keller. With his size and his sort of shambling gait, he suddenly reminded me of a bear, especially in that wild setting. He appeared to be cutting through the garden on his way to somewhere else, because he went into one of the doors on the far side and disappeared.

Movement on the other side of the atrium caught my eye. Directly across from me on the third floor, I saw a man and a woman step out onto their balcony. There was a dim light in the room behind them, shining on the woman's blond hair. She wore a long, slinky, sexy blue nightgown. It plunged deep enough for me to see the dark valley between her breasts as she rested her hands on the balcony railing.

"Well, somebody's gettin' frisky tonight, at least," I murmured. Feeling like I was intruding, I started to step back into my room and close the curtains.

Then the woman across the way half-turned, and the light was behind her head so that I could make out the broad jaw. Callie Madison, I thought. Obviously she had made up with Jake.

Then the man stepped out of the shadows and took Callie's hand to lead her back into the room, and all I could do was stare and mutter to myself, "Well, I'll swan."

Dr. Andrew Jeffords—yeah, the winner of the Orville Redenbacher look-alike contest his own self—took Dr. Callie Madison in that sexy nightgown back into that hotel room, shut the French doors, and closed the curtains, leaving me on the other side of the atrium wondering crazily what the heck was in that popcorn.

CHAPTER 8

This was hardly the first time there had been some hanky-panky going on during one of my tours, of course. Folks who are inclined toward carrying on like that will find a way to do it, even if they're with a bunch of tourists, including their spouse. I'd just as soon have them control their urges, because cheating on your husband or wife has a way of causing all sorts of commotion if the cheated-on partner happens to find out.

Other than that, though, it's really none of my business. Adultery's not like using drugs or getting drunk in public or shoplifting, three other activities that clients sometimes engage in that get my dander up. Nobody's going to get arrested for adultery and cast my agency in a bad light. I'd rather folks not do it, but I can't stop them.

Sometimes, though, the choices people make leave me flabbergasted, and this was one of those times. Callie Madison was young and attractive, and yet there she was, right over there on the other side of the atrium, fooling around with a fella at least thirty years older than her who looked like somebody's kindly old grandpa. Dr. Jeffords had to have some qualities that I had missed.

Then I remembered the comment Tamara Paige had made on the plane about Dr. Jeffords being the head of the English

Department. I didn't know much about university politics, just things that I'd heard Will say, and I wondered if a department head would have enough power to make a subordinate want to sleep with him. One thing I was reasonably sure of: the university would frown on what was happening over there. Enough so that Dr. Jeffords would certainly lose his job, and Callie Madison might, too.

"None of your business, none of your business," I told myself as I closed the French doors and the curtains and started to get ready for bed.

I was still dressed except for my shoes when a knock sounded on my door.

Maybe Will had decided he couldn't stay away from me tonight after all, I thought, as I went to the door and put my eye to the peephole.

But I didn't have to decide what I would do if that turned out to be the case because when I looked through the little lens, I had a nice foreshortened view of Dr. June Powers. She looked upset about something, which made sense, otherwise she wouldn't have been knocking on my door at this time of night.

I turned the deadbolt, unfastened the chain, and opened the door. "Dr. Powers," I said, resisting the impulse to call her Junebug like her father-in-law had. "What can I do for you?"

"Have you seen Papa Larry?" she asked. "I mean, my father-in-law, Dr. Lawrence Powers?"

"Well, I saw him over at the theater, while that reception was going on before the festival's opening ceremonies, but not since then," I told her. "I was just downstairs in the lobby a few minutes ago, and I didn't see him down there."

"I was there, too, as well as at the bar, and I can't find him."

She sounded plenty worried. I couldn't believe the tour had had a second old man go missing on the same night. Not that

84

Dr. Lawrence Powers was anywhere near as old as Howard Burleson. I figured Papa Larry was around sixty, maybe sixty-five.

"I'm sure he's all right," I said. "He's bound to be around the hotel somewhere. Is your husband looking for him, too?"

"Edgar?" June gave a disgusted snort and shook her head. "Edgar is worse than useless in a situation like this, Ms. Dickinson. I didn't even waste the time telling him about it. He'd probably try to run some sort of computer simulation to find his father. If you can't solve it with an equation or a formula, he's not interested."

Her voice had the ragged edge of hysteria in it, to go along with some bitterness and resentment directed toward her husband. I wanted to calm her down, because the last thing I needed was to have another client making a scene tonight. I said, "I'll help you look for him. Just let me get my purse."

I slipped my shoes on, grabbed my bag, and stepped out into the hall. Once I was sure I had my room key card, I let the door close behind me. As we started toward the elevators, I said, "I suppose this has something to do with your father-in-law's drinkin'?"

"What do you mean by that?"

"Well, he wanted a drink on the plane, and you didn't want him to have one. I got the impression that he's under doctor's orders to give it up."

She sighed. "That's right. He's had ulcers and stomach cancer. The cancer is in remission, but he's not supposed to drink. The alcohol could start his stomach bleeding, and . . . and . . ."

"I understand. It could be mighty bad for him."

"He's an old fool!" she said suddenly as we reached the elevators. "He says he'd rather go out on his own terms than have to give up everything that he loves. He says that living like the doctor wants him to is no way for a man to live."

"Somebody ought to have a talk with him."

"Like his son? Yes, it would be nice if Edgar cared enough to do that, wouldn't it? If he could be bothered to try to make his father understand that we love him and want to have him around for as long as possible. Is there any way to quantify that, Ms. Dickinson? Because if there's not, there's no way for Edgar to express it." She jabbed a finger against the elevator button and started to laugh humorlessly. "Have you ever seen the TV show with that scientist who's incredibly smart but has no idea how to interact with the people around him? Well, that's not a situation comedy, Ms. Dickinson. That's a documentary, and it might as well be about Edgar."

Edgar Powers hadn't struck me as being quite that bad, but I didn't really know the man at all. Just like I didn't know his wife or his father. But I was getting to know Junebug a little better than I might have wanted to. I'm not unsympathetic to my clients' personal problems, Lord knows, but I'm not their therapist, either, despite the fact that some of them seem to regard me that way.

The elevator dinged, and the door slid open. "Let's check the bar again," I suggested. "If he wants a drink, that's the most likely place for him to be. Maybe you just missed him."

"Papa Larry's pretty hard to miss," June said. "But I don't suppose it would hurt anything to try."

It was getting close to midnight, but the St. Emilion's bar wouldn't close for a couple of hours yet. It was still pretty crowded. Most of the tables and booths arranged around a horseshoe-shaped bar were occupied. June and I started at one end and began to work our way around to the other. Not everybody in here was from our group, of course, and not all of them were in New Orleans for the literary festival, either. I was aware that some of the men were checking us out, probably wondering if we were going to stop so that they could offer to buy us drinks.

We passed a table where one of the professors was gesturing emphatically as he said, "It's clear that Williams was jealous of Inge, and that's what led to the falling-out between them."

The professor on the other side of the table waved his hands in the air and said, "No one's denying that Williams was jealous of the success Inge's plays had on Broadway during the early to mid-fifties, but it's an overstatement to call the cooling off of their friendship a falling-out. I mean, Inge dedicated *The Dark at the Top of the Stairs* to Williams and suggested to Audrey Wood that Williams write the introduction to the published version."

"Yes, and you've read that introduction. It's clearly not the work of someone who had any affection remaining for Inge."

"But that was all on Williams's side. I believe that Inge still genuinely liked Williams and brought up the subject of writer's block simply out of concern for him."

"I think it's more likely that Inge was deliberately trying to poison the relationship—"

I leaned over the table and said, "Excuse me, boys."

They both looked up at me in surprise.

"Y'all have been arguin' for, what, eight or ten hours straight now, so I reckon you can pick it up again without any trouble. I just need a minute of your time. Do you know Dr. Lawrence Powers?"

"Of course," one of the men responded. "Everybody knows Larry."

"Have you seen him in here tonight?" June asked tensely.

Both men frowned, looked at each other, and then shook their heads. "We've been here ever since we got back from the opening ceremonies," one of them said. "I don't believe Dr. Powers has been in the bar at all."

"I agree," the other one said. "No sign of him." He looked across the table and raised a finger. "But that brings up the interesting point of which director achieved the consistently finest presentation of Williams's work."

And then both of them said simultaneously, "Elia Kazan."

While they were looking shocked that they had found something they couldn't argue about, I said, "Thanks, fellas," and motioned with my head for June to follow me. As we resumed our circuit of the bar, I heard one of them say, "Of course, Kazan's best work was on the screen."

"How can you say that? His stage productions of Williams's plays are clearly superior!"

The rest of the argument was lost—thankfully—in the hubbub of conversation that filled the bar. It took another minute or so for June and me to check out the other tables and booths and the stools along the bar itself. Papa Larry was nowhere to be seen.

The restaurant was closed, so we knew he wasn't in there. June said, "If he wandered off from the hotel, he could be anywhere in the French Quarter. We'll never find him!"

"Now, don't give up yet," I told her. Something obvious occurred to me. "You're sure he's not in his room?"

"I went by there to check just before I came to your room. He didn't answer, and I knocked and called out to him, both."

"Maybe he was in the bathroom, or really sound asleep."

June shook her head. "I'm certain he wasn't there. I knocked for a good five minutes. He would have heard me. And that was the second time I'd been there. I went by earlier to check on him, and he didn't answer the door then, either. That's why I started looking for him."

"You always look in on him like that at night?"

"I do," she said, giving me a defiant frown as if she expected me to try to make something of it. "His health isn't good, and Edgar won't look after him. Somebody has to do it. Anyway, I've gotten in the habit of checking on him every night. We live in the same house, you know."

I hadn't known that and, again, didn't consider it any of my business.

That didn't stop June from going on. "It's the old family home, the house where Edgar grew up. After Lucille passed away—that was Edgar's mother—we moved back there to keep an eye on Papa Larry. He was already in bad health."

"All right, let's try to figure out where else he could be." I didn't want to have to wander around the French Quarter with June at this time of night, poking our heads into every bar and club. That prospect didn't sound appealing at all, or very safe, either.

Something else occurred to me. I said, "Come on," and motioned for June to follow me.

"Where are we going?" she asked as she fell in step beside me.

I started down the corridor toward the garden. "Waiters from the bar circulate through the garden in the atrium."

"I didn't know that."

"So you didn't look there earlier?"

She shook her head. "No. I didn't even think about it."

The garden was a pretty big place, relatively speaking. The hotel took up an entire city block, after all. And there were a lot of trees and shrubs and bushes packed in there, with narrow flagstone paths winding through them. I wondered if it was possible to get lost in there. I pictured a drunken Papa Larry lumbering around, unable to find his way out.

"Should I call his name?" June asked as we started along the first path we came to.

"No, if he's drinkin', he'll know that somebody's lookin' for him and he's liable to hide," I said. "There are tables in here. We'll check them."

"What if he's somewhere in that . . . that jungle?"

I thought about it and said, "If we don't find him at one of the tables, we'll go back upstairs and look down from my balcony. If he's in here, we ought to be able to spot him."

I didn't mention having gazed down at the garden earlier, just before I accidentally spotted Callie Madison and Dr. Jeffords. At that time, the only one I'd seen moving around the garden was Dr. Keller. Dr. Powers could have been at one of the tables then, shielded from my view by its umbrella.

June and I twisted and turned through the garden for a couple of minutes, passing several of the tables where hotel guests sat drinking and talking. At one of the tables, a man and a woman were kissing, but the man wasn't Papa Larry. As we turned a corner around some flowering bushes, I saw a white-jacketed waiter coming toward us, an empty tray tucked under his arm. He smiled and nodded and stepped aside so that we could get past him on the path.

I stopped instead and asked him, "Have you seen a big fella sitting alone at one of the tables in here? He's balding and has a little beard."

He didn't stop smiling as he said, "The hotel staff has a policy of discretion, ma'am—"

"For God's sake," June interrupted. "He's my father-in-law, not some cheating husband. He'll be pouring booze down his throat and he has stomach cancer. It could kill him. Now do you want to talk to me about discretion?"

That shook the smile off the waiter's face. He half-turned and waved the empty tray in the direction we'd been going along the path. "He's up there. I just delivered a rum and cola to him. But I swear I didn't know I wasn't supposed to."

I wanted to tell him that it wasn't his fault, but June didn't look like she was in any mood to be forgiving. I figured we'd better go on and deal with her father-in-law rather than standing around fussing at a waiter, so I just nodded and said, "Thanks. Come on, June."

She glared at the waiter but followed me. We went around a couple more bends in the path, then saw the table in a little open area on the left, with a bright yellow umbrella above it. Dr. Lawrence Powers slouched in a wrought-iron chair that looked like it was bending a little under his weight. He had a half-empty glass in front of him.

"Papa Larry!" June cried.

His bleary eyes widened in surprise as he looked at us. Quickly, he lifted the glass to his lips and guzzled down the rest of the drink, even as June hurried forward to try to snatch it out of his hand. She got the glass, but only after it was empty.

"Too late!" he said triumphantly. "Too late, Junebug!"

"My God, Papa Larry," she said, her voice shaking. "You're drunk."

"Gloriously, uproariously drunk, for the first time in ages! And it feels wonderful, you hear me, wonderful! My brain is fueled and lubricated again, girl. You know a brain as creative as mine can't run on your damned milk!"

"You old fool," she said between gritted teeth. "You're going to kill yourself, you know that, don't you?"

"Then I will die a happy man and go to be with my Lucille." He put both hands flat on the table and went on. "Have you ever been happy, Junebug? Has that cold-blooded son o' mine ever truly made you happy? I don't think so. Leastways, I never heard any evidence of it through the walls at night!"

I had to bite my lip to keep from saying something about how Papa Larry had directed too many Tennessee Williams plays in his time. He was spouting dialogue that sounded like it came from a play, and not a very good one, at that.

But the thing of it was, he was drunk, and somebody who's drunk is usually dead serious. He meant what he was saying, even if he was being overly dramatic about it, and his words found their target, too, because June turned pale with anger and hurt. She said, "Let's get you back up to your room, Papa Larry. You're going to be lucky if you wake up in the morning. We'll need to get you to a doctor tomorrow. I'll call your oncologist in Atlanta and get a referral—"

"I don't need a doctor! I feel fine!"

I said, "We want to keep you feelin' fine, Dr. Powers. It's late, and you need some rest."

"I am a mite tired," he rumbled. He squinted at me. "Who're you again, Red?"

I ignored the nickname and said, "Delilah Dickinson. I'm in charge of the tour."

"Oh, yeah. I 'member you now. How's about helpin' me up?"

June and I got on either side of him and took hold of his arms. I don't know how much he weighed—close to three hundred pounds, surely—but we had to struggle to get him on his feet. He was too drunk to give us much help, but after a minute we managed to get him standing. He took a few unsteady steps down the path with us helping him, then stopped short and said, "Oh, hell. I'm gonna be sick."

He jerked away from us. We couldn't hold him. He lunged to the edge of the path and plowed into the shrubs, parting them with his thick arms. He fell to his knees and started throwing up.

June looked mortified. She muttered, "I'm sorry, I'm sorry."

"Not your fault," I told her. "And not the first sick drunk I've had to deal with on a tour, either."

"I just hope he's not throwing up blood."

"Yeah, you and me both." I had visions of a 9-1-1 call and an ambulance ride to the nearest hospital.

When Dr. Powers was through being sick, June and I started to step off the path to help him up. Before we could reach him, though, he slumped onto his side and lay there motionless. With fear in her voice, June said, "Papa Larry?"

He started snoring.

"You . . . you old fart!" she said. "Now what are we going to do? He's too big for us to lift his dead weight."

"Let's see if we can wake him up enough to help us," I said. I pushed some of the branches aside and moved into the garden, being careful to step around the place where he'd been sick. As I reached Papa Larry's side, I knelt and took hold of his arm, giving it a good shake. "Dr. Powers! Dr. Powers, you need to wake up again for a little while."

Papa Larry kept snoring.

I sighed and shook my head and, as I did, I looked past his bulky shape and saw a shoe sticking out from under a bush. Curious, I moved my head so I could see better and saw a skinny ankle in an argyle sock above the shoe. My heart started to pound harder. Above the shoe and the argyle sock was a trouser leg, and it looked like it went with an old brown suit.

Without thinking too much about what I was doing, I clambered over Papa Larry without disturbing his drunken stupor. I jerked branches aside and saw the rest of the trousers and the suit coat and the bony shape of the man wearing them. I saw a hat lying upside down and then a bald head covered with blood, and then I dropped to my hands and knees next to the body and found myself staring in horror into the dead eyes of Howard Burleson.

93

CHAPTER 9

I was shocked beyond words and for a second I couldn't think straight. Despite what had happened on some of my other tours, my first thought wasn't that the old man had been murdered, but rather that he had wandered out here into the garden, gotten turned around and lost, and in his panic had run into a tree or fallen and hit his head. He had seemed so frail, I didn't think it would have taken much of a blow to finish him off.

But then I saw that there weren't any trees around for him to bash his head against, no rocks or roots he could have landed on. That was when the suspicion started to well up in me. I shook my head and thought, "Not again, not again, not again . . ."

"Ms. Dickinson!" That was June Powers's urgent voice intruding on my thoughts. "Ms. Dickinson, what's wrong? What are you saying?"

I guess I wasn't just thinking that shocked litany; I was saying it out loud. I started to back away from the body. To do that, I had to crawl over Papa Larry again. He was still snoring away.

I pushed myself back to my feet and stumbled out of the bushes. "We . . . we've gotta get some help," I told June.

"He's so drunk you can't wake him up. I knew it." She sighed in exasperation. "I'll go get Edgar. He's not much good for anything, but if you point at something and tell him to pick it up, he can usually manage that. I'd rather not involve the hotel staff unless we have to."

"Oh, they'll have to be involved," I said, "and the police, too."

June stared at me. "The police?" she repeated. "Oh, no, please, Ms. Dickinson, I don't want to have Papa Larry arrested. His health is too bad for that. I'm begging you—"

I held up a hand to stop her. "I'm not talkin' about your father-in-law," I told her. "I'm talkin' about the dead body that's in there beside him."

June's eyes bulged out even more. "D-d-dead body?" she stammered out. "There's a body in there?"

"I'm afraid so."

"Who is it?"

"Howard Burleson."

I could tell she didn't recognize the name right away. Then she thought about it for a couple of seconds and said, "That old man Michael Frasier brought with him? The one who claimed to be one of Tennessee Williams's lovers?"

"Heard about that, did you?"

"I think everybody at the festival has heard about it. Dr. Frasier caused quite a sensation. Which is exactly what he wanted, of course." June shook her head. "And you say he's dead? Could you tell what happened? A heart attack or a stroke, something like that?"

"The cops'll have to figure that out," I said. I didn't want rumors to start spreading and, for all I knew, June might be such a big gossip that she'd go and alert everybody in the hotel to the fact that Burleson was dead. "Go to the front desk and tell them there's an emergency, that we need the police and an ambulance right away." I was almost completely certain that Burleson was dead, but on the slim chance that he wasn't, he needed medical help as soon as possible.

"But . . . but what about Papa Larry?"

A raucous snore came from behind the bushes, as if to answer her question.

"I'll keep an eye on him," I promised. "I'm gonna stay right here until the authorities arrive. Somebody needs to watch the scene and make sure it's not disturbed."

She frowned at me. "You sound like one of those TV cop shows."

I didn't explain to her that I had more experience with homicide investigations than I'd ever wanted to. In fact, if you'd asked me a couple of years ago, I would have said that my desire to be involved in such things was absolutely zero. But they seemed to keep cropping up anyway, whether I wanted them to or not.

"Just go tell 'em at the desk we need help, okay? I'm pretty sure Mr. Burleson's dead, but he might not be."

Understanding dawned on June's face. "Oh. Okay. But don't let anything happen to Papa Larry."

"I won't," I promised.

She turned and hurried off along the path, and the way it twisted through the garden, it was only a few seconds before she was out of sight. That left me standing there alone, except for the guy who was passed out drunk and the bloody corpse of an old man.

That wasn't a very pleasant situation.

It got even more worrisome when I realized that I didn't know how long Burleson had been dead. I had been too shocked to check for a pulse, so I hadn't touched his body. He might have still been warm.

If that was the case, then it was possible that whoever killed him was still close by.

That thought made me glance around nervously, but of course I couldn't see anything except the plants that surrounded me and the path that led through them. Larry Powers made a burbling noise and stopped snoring. That got me to worrying that he had stopped breathing as well, and even though I told myself I was sure he was all right, I really wasn't. I had promised June I would look after him, and I sure as heck didn't want to have two clients die on this tour.

So I took a deep breath, then turned around and pushed my way into the bushes again. I only had to go a couple of steps before I could see Papa Larry again. I looked at him intently until I was sure that his chest was still rising and falling. I didn't want to go any closer because then I would have had an even better look at Burleson's corpse.

Once I was certain that Powers hadn't died in his sleep, I felt a little better. I had started to back out of the bushes when I saw something move ahead of me. Curiosity made me stop and look closer. The gaps in the plant life lined up just right for me to be able to peer through the bushes to the path on the far side where Howard Burleson lay. All I could see was a narrow slice of it, but as I watched, I saw a figure moving away from me at an angle, then disappearing. Maybe it was the circumstances, but something about the person struck me as furtive, even as I recognized the blond hair.

Callie Madison had good reason to be skulking around, I thought. She was cheating on her husband and didn't want him to find out about it.

But was she also a murderer?

I couldn't stop my thoughts from traveling along that trail. I didn't know what room the Madisons were in, but I could find out. If it was on the same side of the hotel that my room was on, she could have taken one of the other elevators down from Dr. Jeffords's room, then cut across the garden to take one of the main elevators back up to her room.

Of course, she could have just gone around the corridor that encircled the atrium and gotten back to her room that way, if it was on the same floor. But she would have been more likely to run into someone she knew that way, and by now it was after midnight. If some of the other professors saw her, it was possible that one of them might say something to Jake about it, and then he would want to know where she had been. I was guessing that he'd been asleep when she slipped out of their room.

But by cutting through the garden to the main elevators, if Jake heard about it, she could make some plausible excuse about going down to the lobby. I supposed the front desk in the St. Emilion, like most hotels, had a supply of tooth-brushes, razors, etc., the sort of things that people sometimes forget when they pack, or lose along the way during a trip. If she told Jake she had gone after something like that, he might wonder about it, but he probably wouldn't be too suspicious.

Of course, all that was just a theory, and maybe a farfetched one at that. One thing I had learned in recent years, though, was that life could be pretty farfetched at times, especially where murder was concerned.

Did I really think that Callie Madison could have killed Howard Burleson? I couldn't think of any reason in the world why she would have . . . but I never would have suspected her of playing around with Dr. Jeffords, either.

It was more likely, though, that she might have seen something that would provide a clue to the real killer. The police would have to talk to her.

Which meant she'd have to explain what she'd been doing down here in the garden at this time of night, and Jake was bound to find out about it, and more than likely her marriage would be ruined. "Shoot," I muttered to myself. Seeing Callie had put me in a bad position. I didn't want to conceal the fact that I'd seen her from the cops. For one thing, the sooner this case was cleared up, the better, and Callie might have vital information.

Of course, said a little voice in the back of my head, I could always talk to her first, before I told the cops anything about her being in the vicinity of the murder . . .

"You're crazy," I told that little voice. I'd had plenty of trying to solve crimes. I wasn't cut out for it, no matter what Will seemed to believe.

But I couldn't stop my thoughts from replaying everything that had happened tonight. I had seen Dr. Ian Keller down here, too, I remembered. That was earlier, but I didn't have any idea how long Burleson had been dead. Keller was big enough and intimidating enough to cast in the role of a murderer a lot easier than Callie Madison was.

Again, though, I couldn't come up with any reason why Dr. Keller would have done such a thing. He didn't have any stake in whether an old man lived or died.

I could think of two people who did, though: Michael Frasier and Tamara Paige.

Before I could ponder on that anymore, I heard hurried footsteps coming toward me. It sounded like several people, so I wasn't surprised when Dale Gillette came around the corner in the path, followed by June Powers and a couple of security guards probably summoned from the hotel's parking garage.

"Oh, my God," Gillette said. "Where is he? Where's the body?"

He still wore his suit and tie and looked as dapper as ever. I couldn't help but ask, "Don't you ever go home?"

"I am home," he snapped. "I live in the hotel. Now take us to the body."

"Right back here," I said, pushing some branches aside.

Gillette shouldered past me and stopped beside Larry Powers.

"Not him," I said. "He's just drunk and passed out. The other one, right there on the other side of that bush."

"Oh." Gillette leaned over and took a closer look, then said in a shaky voice, "Oh, Lord. He looks dead, all right."

One of the security guards said, "Let me check. I used to be a paramedic."

He stepped around Powers and dropped to one knee beside Burleson. It didn't take him long to check for a pulse and not find one. As the guard looked up at us, he shook his head and said, "Sorry, Mr. Gillette. The old guy's dead, all right. The police will still want an ambulance to transport him, though, so it's good that you called for one."

"There's nothing good about this," Gillette said, sounding stricken. "This is terrible, just terrible. Roy, can you tell, did he fall and hit his head or something?"

The security guard leaned over to take a better look at Burleson's head without touching him, and when he looked up this time, his expression was grim. "Nah, he didn't hit his head. Somebody hit it for him."

Gillette frowned. "What are you talking about?"

"His head's bashed in, Mr. Gillette. Somebody killed him."

Gillette staggered, literally staggered. "Killed him?" he repeated. "You mean . . . murdered him?"

"Yeah. This is a homicide. I saw plenty of 'em when I was an EMT."

Gillette started backing away as if he couldn't stand to be that close to the body. He was about to trip over the still-sleeping Larry Powers when I took hold of his arm to keep him from falling.

"Careful," I told him.

He turned to look at me, and the dapper, self-assured young man he'd been earlier transformed into a scared kid just a year or so out of Cornell.

"This can't be murder," he said. "It just can't be."

"You're bound to have had guests die in the hotel before. It's not that uncommon."

"Yeah, there have been a few in the time I've been here, but . . . but they were natural causes. And one drug overdose. Not . . . not murder. This is going to be terrible for the St. Emilion's reputation."

It wasn't going to do wonders for my agency, either, I thought, especially considering the things that had happened on some of my previous tours. But at the moment I couldn't let myself think about that. An old man had been killed. The only thing that mattered right now was finding out who murdered him.

Roy, the security guard who had been a paramedic, turned to Papa Larry. "What about this guy?" he asked. "What's wrong with him?" Before anybody could answer, he leaned over, took a whiff, and said, "Never mind. I can smell the booze."

"He's sick," June put in. "He's had stomach cancer. He's supposed to be in remission, but he shouldn't be drinking."

Roy frowned. "No, he shouldn't. Is he the one who threw up over there?"

"Yeah," I said.

"Well, I don't see any blood in it, that's good. Maybe we'd better get him out of here. Doug, give me a hand."

The other security guard stepped forward, and they each took hold of one of Papa Larry's arms. They hadn't even started trying to lift him, though, when somebody said, "Hold it! What are you doing there?"

I looked up and saw a couple of men in suits on the path. Several uniformed police officers were behind them. The two men looked like detectives, which surprised me. I'd figured that patrol officers would get here first.

"Who's in charge here?" asked the man who had just spoken. He was a rawboned white man with a shock of red hair. His partner was black, tall, and slender with glasses perched on his nose.

"I . . . I guess I am," Gillette replied. "I'm the assistant manager of the hotel. Dale Gillette."

"Has the manager been notified, Mr. Gillette?" the other detective asked.

"Not yet. I wanted to be sure what the situation was first."

"We'll take care of that, then. All communications will flow through us. I'm Detective Nesbit." He inclined his head toward the redhead. "This is Detective Ramsey."

Ramsey gave us a curt, unfriendly nod. He was obviously in a bad mood, which didn't bode well for things going smoothly. Detective Nesbit seemed to be okay, though . . . or maybe they were just already doing the old good cop, bad cop bit. It seemed sort of early for that to me, but maybe that was the way they played everything, right from the start.

"Step away from the body," Ramsey told the two security guards. "You'd better be glad we got here in time to stop you from disturbing our corpse."

"That's not your corpse," I said. "The dead man's over there." I pointed to where Burleson's foot stuck out from behind the bush.

Ramsey glared at me and jerked his chin toward Papa Larry. "Then what's wrong with him?"

"Passed out drunk," Roy said.

"He in any danger of choking or anything like that?"

Roy shrugged. "Doesn't appear to be. He's breathing all right, at least as far as I can tell."

"All right, leave him right where he is for now. It's bad

enough all you people have been trampling around here for God knows how long, messing up our forensics. Nobody move until I tell you it's all right, okay? You . . . Gillette . . . what's the story here?"

Gillette shook his head. "I really don't know, Detective. It was that woman who summoned me out here." He sounded like he was getting some of his aplomb back, but he still looked like a scared little boy as he pointed to June Powers.

Ramsey turned his head to look at her. "Who are you?"

"I'm Dr. June Powers," she said. "And that man lying there is Dr. Lawrence Powers, my father-in-law."

"You mean the drunk guy or the dead guy?"

June looked scared and mad at the same time. "The man who's passed out. He's very ill, by the way."

"Yeah, well, we'll see to it that he gets medical attention if he needs it. So tell us how you found the body."

June shook her head. "But I didn't find the body. She did."

You guessed it. Her finger was pointing at me. Ramsey and Nesbit both looked at me, and Nesbit asked, "What's your name, ma'am?"

"Delilah Dickinson," I told him. He had taken a notebook from inside his coat and started writing names in it. He added mine to the list. Then he looked up with a slight frown.

"That name is familiar."

Ramsey told one of the uniformed cops, "Call it in and have 'em run the name through the databases. Dickinson, Delilah."

"No, that's not it," Nesbit said, shaking his head. "I know I've heard that name before. . . . Where are you from, Ms. Dickinson?"

"Atlanta," I said with a sinking feeling.

A smile suddenly lit up Nesbit's face. "I knew it!" he said. "The *Gone With the Wind* murder!"

CHAPTER 10

Ramsey turned to stare at his partner. "The what?" he asked.

"The *Gone With the Wind* murder," Nesbit repeated, although I'd just as soon not have had to hear that phrase again. "I read about it a couple of years ago. A tour group was visiting one of those plantations near Atlanta where they put on sort of a reenactment of *Gone With the Wind*. Somebody got murdered, and the lady who was running the tour group figured out who the killer was and solved the case." He pointed at me. "Her."

Ramsey turned toward me again. "Is that right?"

I shrugged. "I was there. I don't know how much I did to actually solve anything—"

"And then last year there was something else," Nesbit broke in. "Something about a riverboat. I don't remember the details, but I know there was another murder—"

"Sounds like a Black Widow situation to me," Ramsey said.

"No, no, she's more like that old lady on TV who solves all the murders. I mean, that show was before my time, but I've seen some episodes in reruns."

I didn't know what bothered me more about what Nesbit had just said, but I shoved it all aside. "Look, fellas, this is your case. I just happened to be here."

Ramsey gave his partner an ugly grin. "Well, ain't that nice of the lady? She's gonna let us solve this homicide on our own."

Nesbit ignored that and said, "So you're the one who found the body, Ms. Dickinson?"

I nodded. "Yeah, I guess so."

"How did that come about? Start at the beginning, please, and tell us everything you can remember, whether it seems important or not. Start with how you know the victim."

"Well, I'd never met Mr. Burleson before this morning," I began. "Or rather, yesterday morning, I guess it would be, technically, since it's after midnight—"

"Yeah, we got that," Ramsey broke in. "Get on with it."

I did, telling them about how the tour group had gathered at the airport in Atlanta to fly here to New Orleans for the Tennessee Williams Literary Festival. I explained about Burleson accompanying Dr. Michael Frasier because he'd supposedly been acquainted—intimately acquainted—with Tennessee Williams. I even told them about Burleson's claim to have written *Cat on a Hot Tin Roof*, and as June Powers listened to that, her eyes widened.

"That's ludicrous," she interrupted to say. "There's never been the slightest hint that anyone else was involved in the writing of Williams's plays, other than the first one he wrote while he was in college. He collaborated with another student on that one."

"Skip the lecture, Professor," Ramsey said. "Go on, Ms. Dickinson."

I told them the quick version of everything else that had happened, except for a couple of things. I didn't say anything about seeing Callie Madison on the balcony with Dr. Jeffords, and when Nesbit asked me if I had seen anyone else in the garden around the time I discovered the body, I mentioned seeing Dr. Keller, as well as a blond woman, but I didn't tell them that I had recognized Callie. I still couldn't believe she'd had anything to do with Burleson's death, so I wanted to talk to her first. I hoped that decision wouldn't come back to haunt me.

Explaining how I'd come to find the body was easy. I just told the two detectives exactly what had happened and didn't hold anything back about that. It wasn't until I noticed June looking nervous that I realized what must be going through her mind: drunk or not, Larry Powers had been out here in the hotel garden around the time of Burleson's death. The cops would probably consider him a suspect, too, along with Dr. Keller and the blond woman I hadn't named.

Of course, there could have been a dozen other people in this miniature jungle around that time, I thought. It was designed for privacy. Just because I hadn't seen them didn't mean they weren't there. I was sure Nesbit and Ramsey would question the waiters who'd been delivering drinks out here and try to track down everyone who had been around the scene.

It was harder to answer when Nesbit asked, "Do you know of any enemies the victim might have had? Anyone who might have had a grudge against Mr. Burleson?"

"He seemed like a perfectly harmless old man to me," I said with a frown. "I don't know anyone who would have wanted to kill him. Maybe he stumbled into a drug deal or something."

Ramsey frowned back at me. "Right here in the middle of one of the fanciest hotels in town?"

Actually, I didn't think that possibility was all that likely, either. But it wasn't impossible, and I preferred to think that the crime was one of random violence rather than something connected to my tour group.

Then June blurted out, "What about Tamara?"

"Who?" Nesbit asked.

"Dr. Tamara Paige. She was very upset about the whole idea that the old man might have been one of Tennessee Williams's lovers. She rejected it wholeheartedly."

I glared at June, but I understood what she was doing. She was trying to throw Tamara under the bus in order to divert suspicion from her father-in-law. I suppose I could understand that motivation, but I didn't think either Dr. Paige or Papa Larry was capable of murder.

Then I reminded myself that you never truly know what another person is capable of under the right circumstances. That was a lesson I had learned the hard way.

Nesbit made a note of Tamara's name. Clearly, he was the note-taker of the team. Ramsey hadn't written down anything yet, hadn't even brought out a notebook.

"Did this Dr. Paige make a stink on the airplane?" Ramsey asked.

June nodded eagerly. The detectives had switched all their attention from me to her, and she seemed to be almost enjoying it. "She certainly did," June said, "and then this evening, at the festival's opening ceremonies, it was Dr. Paige who Dr. Frasier accused of doing something to the old man."

"Doing something?" Nesbit repeated. "You mean Dr. Frasier knew then that something had happened to Mr. Burleson?"

"You're gettin' it turned around," I told him. "That was when Mr. Burleson was missing, but we found him."

"Missing?" Ramsey snapped. "The old man went missing?"

"I told you about how Dr. Frasier came to the theater looking for him," I said.

"Yeah, but you didn't make it clear that Frasier already suspected foul play even then," Nesbit said. "Or that Dr. Paige was his leading suspect."

"But nothing had happened to Mr. Burleson then," I said as I realized I must have glided over some of that without really meaning to. Maybe subconsciously I'd been trying to protect Tamara. I don't know. But I went on. "We found him in Petit Claude's, a jazz club around the corner."

Nesbit nodded. "I know the place. When you say 'we,' who do you mean?"

"It was me and my friend, Dr. Will Burke, along with Dr. Frasier and Dr. Paige. We'd gone from the theater back to the hotel to look for Mr. Burleson, and Mr. Gillette told us he'd spoken to Mr. Burleson about Petit Claude's."

Gillette nodded and spoke up for the first time in a while. "That's right, Detectives. Dr. Paige was with Ms. Dickinson, Dr. Burke, and Dr. Frasier."

Nesbit asked, "Did she make any threats about what she might do to Mr. Burleson when they found him?"

Gillette shook his head. "Oh, no, nothing like that. I did notice that Dr. Frasier was very upset and seemed worried that something might have happened to the old man, though. And he and Dr. Paige didn't seem to get along very well."

"What happened when you found the old man in that club?" Ramsey asked me.

"We sat and talked for a while. That's when he told us about how he supposedly wrote *Cat on a Hot Tin Roof*."

"Was Dr. Paige upset about that claim, too?" Nesbit wanted to know.

June didn't let me answer. She jumped in with, "Of course she was upset. Tamara's thesis was on the origins of that play, and she's always concentrated on it in her published work. A revelation as major as a hidden author would invalidate practically everything she's ever written."

Frasier had said pretty much the same thing several times,

and I was sure that when the cops got around to questioning him, he would say it again, as vehemently as possible.

Nesbit wasn't satisfied, though. He said, "Yes, but you weren't there, Dr. Powers." He turned back to me. "You were, Ms. Dickinson. So tell me . . . was Dr. Paige upset with Mr. Burleson because of these claims he was making? Perhaps even angry with him?"

I shook my head. "She was a little upset, maybe, but not angry. Mainly she just didn't believe what Mr. Burleson was saying. But she was always cordial to him."

June sniffed. "She called him an old fraud at both the hotel and the theater. I heard her."

"Like I said, she didn't believe him, but that doesn't mean she was angry with him. If she was mad at anybody, it was Michael Frasier."

"Why would she be mad at Dr. Frasier?" Nesbit asked quickly, pouncing on that.

I sighed. There was no point in trying to hide the relation-ship Tamara had had with Frasier. Will knew about it, and I figured most of the other professors in the group did, too. If I didn't say anything, June would. She had really warmed up to the idea of pointing fingers at Tamara, and I could understand why. The detectives seemed to have lost all interest in Papa Larry.

"Dr. Paige thought that Mr. Burleson was either delusional or lying about knowing Tennessee Williams, in order to get at-tention," I said. "She thought Dr. Frasier was taking advan-tage of him and was going to wind up embarrassing Mr. Burleson, along with himself. And there was some friction be-tween her and Dr. Frasier to start with."

"Because . . . ?" Ramsey prompted.

"From what I hear, the two of them used to be a couple."

June nodded. "That's true. They dated for several months."

"But not anymore?" Nesbit said.

"No, they broke up." June lowered her voice a little and added, "And from what I hear, it was an ugly split, too."

Ramsey and Nesbit both nodded, and I knew that Tamara had moved to the top of their list of suspects. That she was a killer still seemed unlikely to me, but I had to admit to myself that I had known her for less than twenty-four hours. I really didn't know how far she would go to protect a body of work that was threatened by Burleson's claims, as well as to get back at a former boyfriend.

"I take it all these people are staying here at the St. Emilion?" Nesbit said.

I nodded. "That's right."

"I can get you their room numbers," Gillette offered.

"Yeah, we'll need 'em," Ramsey said. "As soon as the crime scene techs get here, we'll start our canvass."

"You're gonna question everybody tonight?" I said. "It's after midnight."

"I think murder's enough to justify waking them up, don't you?" Ramsey said, and I didn't like his smirk or his nasty tone of voice. He was right, though, and I knew it. The sooner they could question everybody, the greater the odds that they would be able to find the killer.

It was at that moment that Larry Powers groaned, rolled onto his back, and said, "Wha . . . wha . . . what the hell . . ." He tried to lift his head so he could look around, but he couldn't make it. He just groaned again and let his head fall back.

Nesbit moved over to him and knelt at his side. "Dr. Powers, can you hear me? Do you understand what I'm saying?"

Papa Larry kept his eyes squeezed tightly shut. "Make the hotel . . . stop spinning," he said. "I don't wanna be . . . sick again."

I wasn't sure he had anything left in his stomach to throw

111

up, but I didn't figure pointing that out would do any good, so I kept quiet. Nesbit motioned to the two hotel security guards and said, "Let's get him sitting up."

Ramsey said, "He's probably too drunk to answer any questions."

"I'm not . . . drunk," Larry protested. "I'm . . . sick."

I thought he was some of both, but again, I kept that to myself. The guards got on either side of him and each took an arm. As they lifted him, Nesbit put a hand behind his neck to steady him. Between them, they managed to get Larry upright, although still a long way from being on his feet.

"Who the hell are you?" he asked Nesbit. Blinking in confusion, Larry looked around at Ramsey and the other cops, then at me, Gillette, and June. "What the hell's goin' on here, Junebug?"

She opened her mouth to answer, but Nesbit held up a hand to stop her. "Just talk to me right now, Dr. Powers," he said. "I'm Detective Nesbit of the New Orleans Police Department. Can you tell me what you were doing out here in the hotel garden?"

"Cops?" Larry said with a frown. He looked at June. "You called the cops on me just because of a little drinkin', Junebug?" Then his gaze swung over to me. "No! I bet it was you, Red. What was your name again?"

"Dr. Powers, please listen to me," Nesbit said. "You're not in trouble. No one called the police about your drinking. Is that what you were doing out here?"

Larry belched, then lifted a trembling hand and drew the back of it across his mouth. "Y-yeah," he said. "I wanted a drink, so I . . . came out here. Didn't think anybody would . . . see me. I'm not . . . supposed to drink."

"I'll say you're not," June put in. "You could have killed

yourself, you . . . you old fool! You may have done irreparable damage to your stomach."

Larry shook his head. "It doesn't . . . feel that bad. Just a little . . . queasy."

"Dr. Powers," Nesbit pressed on, "did you see anyone out here?"

"When?"

"Earlier, while you were drinking."

"Just the waiter. He came by . . . a few times . . . brought me some booze."

"What about sounds? Did you hear anyone arguing?"

Larry frowned and pouted at the same time, making him look like a big, goateed baby. "I don't like this. I don't feel good. I want to go to my room and lie down."

"We'll see about letting you do that in a few minutes," Nesbit promised. "First, though, you need to concentrate and tell me if you saw or heard anything unusual out here before you passed out."

Larry sat there for a long moment, then shook his head. "I don't remember anything. I don't even remember passing out. The last thing I recall is sitting at a table with a rum and cola."

June said, "You don't even remember when Ms. Dickinson and I found you? You talked to us."

"Maybe so, but it's gone now." He looked around at all of us. "Nobody's told me what's going on here. If you didn't call the cops about me, what are they doing here? Why all the questions?"

"Look behind you, Dr. Powers," Nesbit suggested quietly.

Larry was a big guy with a fat neck. He had trouble turning his head. But when he finally managed to do so, he saw the lower half of Howard Burleson's body and flinched away from it as a shocked expression appeared on his face.

"Whoa! What the hell! Who's that? Is he hurt?"

His surprise seemed genuine, but I recalled what he had just said about not remembering the conversation he'd had with June and me. Maybe something else had happened that he didn't remember. Maybe he had run into Howard Burleson out here in the garden. I couldn't think of any motive for Larry Powers to bash in the old man's head, but Larry had been pretty drunk. Maybe Burleson had said something that made him mad. I didn't know what sort of temper Larry had. June would know that better than I would . . . and she had been doing her best to cast suspicion anywhere else. Maybe that meant something.

"That's Howard Burleson," Nesbit said. "Do you remember seeing him or talking to him, Dr. Powers?"

"The old-timer that Michael Frasier brought with him? I saw him on the plane and as we were checking into the hotel, but those are the only times."

"That you remember," Ramsey said with a harsh edge in his voice.

"Of course that I remember," Larry snapped. "I can't tell you anything I don't remember, now can I?"

"Do you know of anybody who would have a reason to hurt Mr. Burleson?" Nesbit asked.

Larry lowered his voice to a half-whisper. "Is he dead? He's not moving."

"Yes, sir, he's dead," Nesbit replied with a solemn nod. "Do you have any idea why anyone would want to kill him?"

"He seemed like a harmless old man to me. It doesn't make sense that anyone would want to . . . to hurt him." Evidently Larry couldn't bring himself to use the word "kill." He frowned again and looked up. "Unless . . ."

"Unless what?" Ramsey demanded when Larry's voice trailed off.

"Well . . . I hate to say it . . . but Dr. Paige seemed really upset about the whole thing. I think that was just because Mike Frasier was involved in it, though. She really couldn't stand him after they broke up."

Nesbit had been kneeling beside Larry while the questioning was going on, but now he stood up. "Let's leave the officers here to secure the scene," he suggested to Ramsey. "I think it's time we go talk to Dr. Tamara Paige."

CHAPTER 11

"What about the rest of us?" I said. "Are we free to go?"

"Don't leave the hotel," Nesbit said. "But yes, I suppose we're through with you for now."

"We'll have men on all the exits," Ramsey added. "So don't try to sneak out."

I thought his suspicious tone of voice was a little uncalled-for, but he was a detective, after all, I reminded myself. It was his job to be suspicious.

On the other hand, his real job was to clear the cases assigned to him, and I knew that in order to do that, some cops decided as quickly as possible on the most likely suspect and focused all their efforts on that one person. A lot more times than not, of course, they were right and the most likely suspect was guilty. Most crime was pretty basic and simple.

But not all of it, and sometimes the real culprit got away with what he'd done because the police paid too much attention to one suspect and pretty much ignored the others. I was afraid that in this case, Tamara Paige was becoming that one major suspect, if she wasn't already.

Ramsey crooked a finger at Gillette and went on, "Come with us. We'll need a printout of all the guests you have staying in the hotel tonight, especially the ones who belong to the same tour group as the victim."

"I can get you that," Gillette said with a nod, obviously eager to please. He wanted the cops—and the trouble—out of his hotel as quickly as possible.

"Before you go," June said, "can someone help me with my father-in-law? I'd like to get him back up to his room."

Gillette looked at the security guard named Roy, the one who had been a paramedic. "Do you think it's all right to move him, or should a doctor check him out first?"

"Don't ask me. I'm not an EMT anymore."

"No, but you know more about it than any of the rest of us," Gillette insisted. He glanced at the detectives. "If that's all right with you, Officers . . ."

Ramsey shrugged, and Nesbit said, "Sure, go ahead."

Roy sighed and knelt beside Larry Powers again. "Let me have your wrist, sir," he said.

He took hold of Larry's wrist for a moment, then nodded and said, "Pulse is good. He seems to be breathing all right." He held up a finger in front of Larry's face and moved it from side to side. "Follow this with your eyes. Don't turn your head."

After another minute or so, Roy reported, "He's still about half drunk, but I think he'll be okay. No sign of concussion or anything like that. Any unusual pains, sir?"

"No," Larry said. "Actually, I feel pretty good right now, considering."

Roy grunted. "I doubt if that'll be the case in the morning. But you're all right to move now, in my opinion . . . which, legally, isn't worth a damned thing, I want to remind everybody. If you move this man, it's your responsibility, not mine."

"All right, get him on his feet," Ramsey ordered. "We've got things to do."

With help from Gillette, Roy and the other guard lifted Larry. He was pretty shaky, but he wasn't in as bad a shape as he had been earlier when June and I were first helping him. June must have realized that, because she said, "Ms. Dickinson and I can take care of him from here."

I didn't really appreciate being volunteered like that, but I'd been willing to help with Larry earlier, so I supposed it wouldn't hurt me now. If I tripped over another dead body on our way up to his room, though, I was swearing off good deeds forever.

We flanked Larry like the guards had done and each took an arm. He started moving his feet in a somewhat haphazard manner that somehow propelled him forward. As we moved off along the path, I glanced back. I couldn't see Burleson's body now because of the bushes and shrubs, but I knew it was back there, lying still and forlorn in death. Whatever the old man had done in his life, whether his wild story about writing *Cat on a Hot Tin Roof* was true or not, he hadn't deserved to come to such a brutal end.

Gillette, Nesbit, and Ramsey headed for Gillette's office to get those room numbers and other information. June and I stopped at the elevators with Larry. At this time of night, well after one o'clock now, it didn't take long for one of the elevators to open up when June pressed the button. We stumbled into it with Larry. I was on the side of the car where the controls were located, so I asked, "Which floor are you folks on?"

"Second," June replied. I jabbed a finger against that button on the control panel.

Larry's room was about halfway along the corridor toward the corner of the building. That seemed a lot farther than it really was when you were trying to make sure that a three-hundred-pound drunk didn't fall flat on his face with every step.

When we finally reached the door, June asked a question that maybe we should have thought about earlier. "Larry, you do have your key, don't you?"

"I . . . I dunno," he said. He turned his head toward me and leered. "Why don't you check my pockets, Red?"

"Check 'em yourself," I told him, keeping a tight rein on my temper.

"Yes, Papa Larry, if we let go of you, you're liable to fall down," June said. "Just look in your pockets."

Larry complied, although he had to check several of the pockets more than once before he came up with the key card. But then he held it up triumphantly and said, "There's the little rascal! I knew it had to be in there somewhere."

I was closer, so I kept one hand under his elbow and used the other to take the key out of his fingers and swipe it through the reader on the door handle. The indicator light turned green. I turned the handle and swung the door open.

"All right, Papa Larry," June said. "We're here at your room. Let's go on in now."

The door wasn't wide enough for the three of us to go through side by side. June tried to turn sideways and go through first, but Larry jerked loose from us and slapped his hands on either side of the door.

"I can manage by myself, damn it," he rumbled. He had reached that inevitable stage of drunkenness where he was turning surly.

He tried to take a step through the doorway but reeled against the jamb instead. He cursed bitterly as he grabbed at the wall to keep himself from falling.

The door of the next room along the corridor opened and Edgar Powers stepped out with a frown on his face. He still wore the trousers from his suit and a white shirt, but he had taken off his coat, tie, and shoes, anyway.

"June?" he said. "I wondered where you were. What's going on out here? Dad, what's wrong with you?"

June's voice was icy as she said, "So, you finally looked up from your computer and realized that I never came back from checking on Papa Larry. Edgar, I left the room nearly two hours ago!"

"I was busy working on some simulations with Dr. Shinobi from the University of Tokyo," Edgar explained. "It's already morning over there." He frowned. "Is my dad okay?"

"No, he's not okay. He got drunk!"

Edgar's frown deepened as he shook his head. "That's not good. His doctor said—"

"We all know what my damn doctor said!" Larry roared. "Somebody give me a damn hand here!"

June motioned to Edgar, who came over and took hold of his father's arm. With some effort, the two of them managed to get through the door and on into the room. June and I followed as Edgar led Larry to the side of the bed and helped him sit down. As soon as Edgar let go and stepped away, Larry toppled over backward and moaned.

"I'll get his shoes off of him, at least," Edgar said, his face grim now. "He may have to sleep it off in his clothes, though."

He had bent down and was working on Larry's shoes when June and I stepped back out into the hall. Fancy windows on the other side of the corridor showed the lights of the French Quarter glittering in the night, and it would have been pretty under other circumstances.

June crossed her arms and sighed. "Thank you for your help, Ms. Dickinson. I never would have gotten through this horrible evening if it weren't for you. I might not have found Papa Larry, and there's no telling what might have happened to him."

That was true. If Howard Burleson's murderer had still been

close by, he might have killed Larry, too, to eliminate a potential witness, if June and I hadn't come along when we did. The killer might have balked at trying to get rid of all three of us. And that didn't even take into account the possibility that if we hadn't found him, Larry might have kept guzzling down the booze until he'd drunk himself to death.

"I'm here to help," I told June. "That's my job. But I'd just as soon not have to deal with any more drama."

"Or dead bodies." A shudder went through her.

"Yeah. One of those is more than enough."

Edgar came out of the room and eased the door closed behind him. "All right, I got his shoes off and rolled him all the way up onto the bed," he reported. "That's the best I can do. He went to sleep right away. How in the world did he manage to get drunk?"

"How do you think?" June snapped. "He went downstairs, hid out in that garden in the middle of the atrium, and had waiters bring him drinks from the bar."

Edgar sighed. "That stubborn old man. He knows better."

"Maybe you should have a talk with him."

Edgar shook his head at that suggestion. "He won't listen to me. You know that, June."

"So you just give up trying? Is that it? Just like you gave up on our marriage?"

"What? I never gave up on our marriage!"

That bitter exchange was my cue to slip away. This argument sounded like one they'd had before.

I had started to back away when June said, "Wait a minute, Ms. Dickinson. Wouldn't you call it giving up when a man spends almost every waking minute on his work and has to be dragged off on a vacation, even a trip like this one that's mostly work?"

I held up my hands. "You folks better just leave me out of

this. My job's to get folks where they're goin' and keep the trip runnin' smooth."

Which it sure hadn't done so far, I thought.

"You're supposed to keep the members of your group happy, right?" June demanded.

"Well . . . I suppose."

"Do I seem happy to you?"

Edgar said, "I don't understand. I do everything you ask me to do."

She gave him a withering glare. "My God, Edgar, you didn't even notice that I never came back to the room in the middle of the night! Something could have happened to me. I could have been mugged. I . . . I could have met some other man and gone off to bed with him! Did you ever even think about that?"

To be fair to Edgar, that last possibility probably wouldn't have occurred to me, either, at least not right away.

"I did notice you were gone," he insisted. "When I heard your voices out here in the hall, didn't I come out right away to check and see what was going on?"

"Yes, and how long before that was it that you noticed?" she shot back.

"I don't know." He shrugged. "Awhile."

"And you didn't come to look for me, did you?"

"I told you, I was working with Dr. Shinobi, and I was sure you'd be back eventually—"

That was the wrong thing to say. June said, "Oh!" and turned to stalk off down the hall toward the elevators.

"Where are you going?" Edgar called after her.

"I don't know! I'll sit up in the bar all night if I have to, before I'll go back into that room with you!"

He looked at me. "Ms. Dickinson, isn't there something you can do?"

"Yeah, there is," I told him. "I can go back to my room and try to get some sleep while you folks sort out your own troubles."

I left him there, staring after me helplessly as I walked off. He needed more help than I could give him.

June was still waiting for an elevator to take her downstairs. I pushed the button for one going up.

"Did you ever see such a clueless, insensitive—"

"Yes," I told her.

"I think all men must be like that."

I thought about Will and my friend Mark Lansing and my son-in-law, Luke, and I said, "No, not all of them. Some of them are good guys. Maybe not most of them, but some."

"Well, I certainly never met any. Edgar's hopeless. And Papa Larry's just as bad in different ways—he always caroused around and neglected his wife and family. He was just as obsessed with the theater and the plays he was directing as Edgar is with his work." One of the elevators dinged, and the down indicator lit up. "You want to come down to the bar and have a drink with me?"

I shook my head. "Thanks, but no thanks. I was just about to get ready to turn in when you knocked on my door awhile ago. I just want to get some sleep."

"Of course. Well, good night, Ms. Dickinson . . . and thanks again." She got into the elevator and pushed the button for the ground floor. "I'm sorry about, well, about the murder."

"Yeah, me, too," I said as the door slid closed, cutting her off from view.

My elevator arrived a moment later, and I rode up to the third floor. As I got off and started down the hall, I heard the rattle of ice cubes coming from an ice machine that was set in a little vending machine alcove. Dr. Tamara Paige stepped out of the alcove and turned toward me, holding the plastic ice bucket from her room.

I hadn't seen her since we all left Petit Claude's. Will and I had gone on to supper, and I supposed Tamara had returned to the hotel. She had changed out of the dress she had worn to the festival's opening ceremonies and now had on sneakers and a leotard with sweatpants over it. The sweat stains on the leotard told me she had been working out.

If anybody had asked me earlier, I would have said that I'd figured she'd come back to the hotel and gone to bed. Obviously, that wasn't the case. I smiled and nodded.

"Ms. Dickinson," she said. "How was your supper with Dr. Burke?"

"Very nice," I told her.

She gave me a sly smile. "You're just now getting back to your room?"

No, I've been busy tripping over a dead body and being interrogated by the cops, I thought, and that made me wonder why Ramsey and Nesbit weren't already up here questioning her. They must have still been down in Gillette's office, gathering that information about the hotel guests. I assumed they would run everyone's names through their computers.

And that left me with a sticky little moral dilemma. I liked Tamara, I didn't believe she was a murderer, and I wanted to warn her that a couple of police detectives would soon be on their way upstairs to question her about Howard Burleson's death, which, from the way she was acting, she didn't know a blasted thing about.

At the same time, I knew that if I told her, and Ramsey and Nesbit found out about it, I could be in fairly serious trouble for obstructing their investigation.

I postponed the decision by saying, "Some other things

came up," then hurrying on, "I thought you would have been asleep by now."

"Oh, I tried," she said. "I just couldn't get that old man's story out of my head, though. I still don't believe him, mind you, but I couldn't stop wondering if he might be telling the truth. And I'm still mad at Michael for starting all this. People are going to laugh at Mr. Burleson, and that's going to hurt him. It's not fair." She shrugged. "So I did what I always do when I have trouble sleeping. I got up and did some tae kwon do. Sometimes a good hard workout clears my head, and then I can sleep."

"So you're one of those martial artists, eh?" In that leotard, I couldn't help but notice the sharply toned muscles in her arms and shoulders. In the clothes she'd been wearing earlier, that hadn't been so apparent. She looked like she was in good enough shape to kick some serious butt.

Or hit an old man hard enough, fast enough, and enough times to shatter his skull.

But that was crazy, I told myself. Tamara was acting like she had no idea Burleson was dead. She had just expressed sympathy for him because she thought Frasier's presentation was going to wind up embarrassing him. Why would she act like that if she had killed the old man earlier?

Maybe *because* she had killed the old man earlier, I thought suddenly. If she was guilty, of course she would act like she didn't know anything about it. To behave any other way would just be foolish.

"I've been doing tae kwon do for years," she answered my question. "My work doesn't give me any exercise, so I had to find some other way to stay in shape, and this seems to work."

It worked all right. She was obviously in good shape. But as far as Detectives Ramsey and Nesbit were concerned, that might just be one more mark against her.

I shouldn't have thought about Ramsey and Nesbit. The elevator opened again a short distance down the hallway, and with heavy footsteps they came down the hall toward us. Tamara glanced toward them and for a second a look of alarm flickered through her eyes. Was that a sign of guilt? Or just a woman's natural reaction when she's standing in a hotel corridor and suddenly sees two grim-faced men in cheap suits striding toward her?

"Ms. Dickinson?" Nesbit said. "What are you doing here?"

"And who's your friend?" Ramsey added with an ominous frown directed at Tamara.

Lying wasn't going to do me any good. I said, "This is Dr. Paige."

"Just the woman we want to see," Nesbit said.

"Yeah," Ramsey agreed. Then he pointed a threatening finger at me and said, "And if you've said anything to her about that murder downstairs, you're under arrest."

CHAPTER 12

Tamara said, "Murder!" and I said, "Arrest!" at the same time, and both words came out like startled yelps.

I wasn't completely surprised by Ramsey's threat, because a similar thought had gone through my head a few moments earlier. Thinking about it, though, and hearing the actual words coming out of an angry police detective's mouth were two mighty different things.

"Take it easy," Nesbit said with a soothing quality in his voice. They were back to the good cop, bad cop bit. "Nobody's being arrested. We just want to ask you a few questions, Dr. Paige."

"Yeah," Ramsey said. "Like what did this meddling red-head tell you?"

Why do men always have to bring up the color of my hair? If I'd been a blonde, a guy might have mentioned that every once in a while, but Ramsey never would have asked, *What did this brunette tell you?* Never in a million years.

I don't know why that crazy thought crossed my head just then, but it did. I ignored it and said, "I didn't tell her anything. We were just making small talk like you do when you run into an acquaintance in a hotel hallway."

Tamara shot me a narrow-eyed look, like maybe she thought

I should have told her what was going on. But she just said, "Who are these men, and what's this about a murder?"

"This is Detective Ramsey and Detective Nesbit from the New Orleans PD," I said, nodding to each of them as I introduced them.

"Go ahead and answer her other question," Ramsey said. "I want to hear how you do it."

I couldn't stop myself from glaring at him for a second before I turned back to Tamara. "Howard Burleson is dead," I said. "His body was found downstairs in that garden in the middle of the atrium a little while ago. Somebody killed him."

Her eyes got big with shock. "My God," she murmured. "That poor old man! But how do you know he was killed? He could have had a heart attack or a stroke—"

"Someone hit him several times in the head," Ramsey broke in. "Possibly with a fist, possibly with a blunt object. Busted it wide open. Blood all over the place."

Tamara paled and took an instinctive step backward. "How awful! I can't imagine anybody doing such a thing. He . . . he was a nice old man."

"For a lying fraud?" Nesbit prodded gently.

Tamara's face hardened. "Wait just a minute. What are you saying? Surely you don't think I had anything to do with what happened to him?"

"From what we've heard so far, it sounds like the victim was going to present some claims at the literary festival that would have threatened to seriously undermine your work, Dr. Paige."

Ramsey ran his gaze up and down her athletic body and added, "You look like you're in pretty good shape, Doctor. Plenty good enough to punch out an old man, anyway."

Tamara started to back away as panic welled up in her eyes. "That's crazy!"

Nesbit took a quick step toward her. "Please, Dr. Paige, stay right where you are."

Tamara started shaking her head. "I'm not going to stand here and listen to this lunacy. I've never hurt anyone. You . . . you can't accuse me of . . . of such a horrible thing!"

"No one's accusing you," Nesbit said. "We just have to ask you some questions—"

"No!" Tamara turned and broke into a run, dropping the ice bucket as she did.

It shocked me that she ran. I would have thought that she was smarter. But maybe she was guilty, I thought, and even if she wasn't, maybe she just lost her head and panicked. But either way, it was a stupid thing to do, as she found out a second later when Nesbit lunged after her, sailed through the air, and tackled her from behind.

They went down hard. Luckily, the thick carpet must have cushioned their fall a little. Tamara cried out as Nesbit landed on top of her. He grabbed her left wrist and dragged it behind her back, then pinned it there with his left hand while he reached for her right wrist. He snagged that one, too, and yanked that arm behind her. Then he held them both in place with one hand while he reached for his cuffs with the other.

Tamara was sobbing by now. I took an instinctive step toward her. Ramsey yelled, "Stay back!" and I looked over to see that he had his gun out. It was an ugly, short-barreled revolver. "Stay back," he told me again, and between the gun and the look on his face, I knew I'd better do what he said.

Nesbit had plastic restraints on Tamara's wrists by now, locking her arms behind her back. He pushed himself up and off of her. Ramsey holstered his gun and hurried forward to help his partner. Each of them grasped one of Tamara's arms, then Nesbit said, "We're going to help you stand up, Dr. Paige. Please don't try to fight us."

Tamara was still sobbing. I didn't think she had any fight left in her.

They got her on her feet and moved her over so that she could lean back against the wall. "Are you all right?" Nesbit asked. "Are you hurt? Do you need medical attention?"

"I . . . I didn't do it," Tamara said, gasping with fear and desperation in her voice. "I didn't hurt anybody."

"Then why'd you run?" Ramsey said.

That was a good question. I wanted to think it was just because she had gotten scared and stopped thinking straight, but I wasn't sure anymore.

"I didn't kill that old man. I've never been accused of such a thing in all my life!"

"Again, no one has accused you," Nesbit said. "You're not under arrest."

I said, "Then why the cuffs?"

Ramsey gave me a dirty look. "Are you her lawyer?"

"You know I'm not."

"Then you don't get to ask questions," he snapped.

Nesbit said, "Dr. Paige is being detained for questioning. That's all."

"She's got a right to have a lawyer," I insisted. "Even if you haven't charged her with anything, she doesn't have to answer questions if she doesn't want to, and she has a right to have an attorney present if she does."

"You've watched too many TV shows, lady," Ramsey told me with a sneer.

"I don't think I'm the only one," I told him. "When you were wavin' that gun around, I kept expectin' you to yell 'Freeze!' "

I know, mouthing off to a cop isn't the smartest thing in the world. Ramsey rubbed me the wrong way, though, and, anyway, I felt a responsibility toward Tamara. She was one of my clients, and I wasn't going to let them mistreat her or take advantage of her.

Ramsey didn't like what I'd said. He clenched his jaw so tight that a little lump of muscle poked out from it. He took a step toward me, but before he could say anything else, Nesbit jumped back in.

"I suppose you're right, Ms. Dickinson," he said. "Don't worry, we'll follow proper procedure. We're going to take Dr. Paige in for questioning, but her rights will be protected. If she wants a lawyer, she'll have one."

I looked at Tamara. "Do you know any lawyers in New Orleans?"

"Of course not!" she replied with a shake of her head. "Why would I?"

"How about back in Atlanta? I could call him for you and see if he can recommend anybody here."

Slowly, she shook her head again. "I have a personal attorney, but I doubt if he would know anybody who could handle something like this. Something like murder!"

"Is that a confession, Doctor?" Ramsey asked with an ugly grin.

"No," Tamara said. "No, it's not a confession at all. I don't need to confess. I haven't done anything wrong."

Ramsey leaned closer to her. "Everybody's done something," he said quietly. "They say confession is good for the soul."

"Come on," Nesbit said. "We'll get some of the patrol officers to continue with the canvass."

Firmly but not roughly, he turned Tamara toward the elevators. "We'll see that you have a public defender if you want one," he went on, as he started marching her along the hall.

Ramsey turned and glared at me. "You're lucky we're not

taking you in, too, Ms. Dickinson. If I were you, I'd go to my room and keep my mouth shut. You don't want to get in the middle of our investigation."

"You got that right, Detective," I said. The look I gave him wasn't any friendlier than the one he was giving me.

He grunted and then followed Nesbit and Tamara. I watched until the three of them got into one of the elevators and headed down.

Maybe Ramsey and I had both been wrong just now, I realized. Despite what I had said about not wanting to get involved, it was too late for that. I was smack-dab in the middle of the mess involving Howard Burleson's murder. How could it be any other way when I had discovered the body? Not only that, but both the victim and the leading suspect were members of my tour group.

Like it or not, I couldn't just turn my back on everything, especially when I wasn't convinced that Nesbit and Ramsey were really after the truth. I thought a quick arrest and a cleared case were the things that mattered the most to them. That was why they had their sights set on Tamara.

It was too late tonight to do anything about it, but first thing in the morning, I vowed, I would have some questions of my own to ask.

And I would start by talking to Dr. Callie Madison.

But if I thought this hellacious night was over, I was wrong. I had been in bed about ten minutes but hadn't dozed off yet when someone pounded on my door. The knocking had an angry sound to it, so I wasn't surprised when I got up, went to the door, looked through the peephole, and saw Dr. Michael Frasier standing in the hallway.

I considered ignoring him, but I figured it was unlikely he

would go away anytime soon. Muttering to myself, I pulled a robe on over my pajamas and then opened the door.

"What?" I snapped before he could say anything.

"Howard Burleson is dead!"

I nodded. "Yeah, I know. I found his body."

"And it didn't occur to you to come and tell me? My entire career was riding on that old man!"

"Maybe you weren't smart to stake so much on a fella who might've dropped dead at any time," I told him. That thought had already occurred to me. Somebody had murdered Burleson, sure, but his age put him at risk to start with. "Did you at least record his story?"

Frasier went from looking angry to looking sick in the blink of an eye. "No," he said miserably. "I didn't think it was necessary. I thought it would be much more effective to have him deliver his claims in person."

"I guess so, but you should have backed them up somehow." I wasn't sure why I was trying to help him, but I thought of something else and went on. "You've got those manuscript pages he said he wrote."

Frasier's eyes lit up. "The *Cat on a Hot Tin Roof* pages! Of course!" His glare came back. "But you still should have come and told me what was going on. My God! The police came and questioned me. I would have appreciated a little warning."

"If I'd warned you, then I would have been in trouble with the law," I pointed out. "The cops ordered me not to say anything to anybody."

"Do you know if they've arrested anybody yet?"

I hesitated. Detective Nesbit had made it clear that Tamara wasn't actually being arrested . . . but by now that situation might have changed. Anyway, they had handcuffed her and taken her with them, and the way most people would look at it, that qualified as an arrest.

But before I could figure out if I wanted to tell Frasier about that, he got an excited look on his face and said, "Wait a minute! I know who must have done it! There's only one person who had anything to gain by killing Howard."

He turned and stalked off down the corridor, and it took me only a moment to realize that he was heading for Tamara's room.

I wasn't sure how he knew which room she was in. I didn't even know that, only that her room was on the same floor as mine. Maybe he'd been stalking her.

I hurried after him and started to tell him that she wasn't there, that the police had hauled her off about a half-hour earlier. But he had already stopped in front of a door and started banging on it the way he'd been banging on mine a few minutes earlier.

When there was no answer, he grabbed the door handle, shook it, and called angrily, "Damn it, Paige, open up! I know you're in there!"

I had stopped about ten feet behind him in the hall. With my arms crossed, I told him, "No, she's not, and you'd better hush before you wake up everybody on this floor."

He turned to stare at me. "What are you talking about?"

I didn't see any way out of telling him the truth. "She's not in there because the police took her in for questioning awhile ago."

"I knew it!" He pumped a fist in the air. "They've already got her!"

"Hold on, hold on. I said they took her in for questioning. She hasn't been arrested." As far as I know, I added to myself.

"It's only a matter of time," Frasier said confidently. "I

know how weak and spineless she really is. She'll crack and confess that she killed Howard to save her own reputation."

Tamara hadn't struck me as weak at all. She seemed plenty strong willed, as well as strong physically. The only way she would confess to Howard Burleson's murder, I thought, was if she'd actually done it.

A door several rooms away opened, and a couple of uniformed police officers stepped out, followed by Will Burke. I remembered that Detective Nesbit had said they would get some uniforms to finish canvassing the hotel guests, and I figured that was what those two officers were doing.

Will wore a bathrobe, too, and his hair was tousled from sleep. I thought he looked cute. I didn't have time to dwell on that, however, because the cops looked at me and Frasier, and one of them demanded, "What's all the racket out—hey, it's that redhead Ramsey told us about!"

Both officers came toward me. The second one said, "What are you doing out here, ma'am? Detective Ramsey warned you about trying to interfere with the investigation that's going on."

"I'm not interferin' in anything," I insisted. I pointed at Frasier. "I just followed Dr. Frasier here to try to keep him from makin' a commotion."

"Well, you didn't do a good job of it," the first cop said. "We heard all that pounding on doors. After we talked to you, Dr. Frasier, didn't we just tell you to stay in your room?"

"Yes, but I thought of something!" Frasier said. "I figured out who killed the old man!"

"You'd better let Detectives Ramsey and Nesbit worry about that. That's their job, Doctor, not yours."

"But I'm telling you, it had to be Dr. Paige!" Frasier thumped a hand against the door of Tamara's room.

"She's already been taken in for questioning," one of the cops said.

"I know. You'd better keep her locked up. She might try to kill me next. She's really got it in for me."

"I'm sure you'll be safe," the other cop said. "We'll have officers here in the hotel the rest of the night."

Frasier nodded. "All right. Those detectives will be making a mistake if they don't go ahead and arrest her for murder, though."

"Just quiet down and go on back to your room, sir. We're trying to disturb the rest of the guests as little as possible."

"Fine," Frasier said. He glanced at me. "I've got to go check on something, anyway. With those manuscript pages, I might still be able to salvage my presentation."

He hurried down the hall. The cops went to the next room, knocked on the door, and were admitted a moment later by one of the professors who'd spent the whole trip so far arguing with his buddy about Tennessee Williams. That left Will and me alone in the hall to look at each other and shake our heads.

"I can't believe it," Will said. "Only a few hours ago we were sitting in Petit Claude's with Mr. Burleson, and he was having such a good time."

"And now he's dead," I said. "It's a real shame. Things happen that way, though."

Especially on my tours, I thought, but I couldn't bring myself to say it.

"What was that about Tamara being taken in for questioning?" Will wanted to know.

I nodded. "It's true. The police seem to think she has the strongest motive, and I don't think she has an alibi. She was alone in her room most of the time after she got back from that club."

"Well, I just don't believe that she killed that old man. I don't think she'd hurt anyone."

"Even to save her career?" I asked, playing devil's advocate for the moment.

Will frowned and was about to answer, probably to defend Tamara again, when a bloodcurdling shriek suddenly sounded from down the hallway.

As best I could tell, it was coming from Dr. Michael Frasier's room.

CHAPTER 13

William and I were closer to Frasier's room than the cops, who popped out into the hall when they heard the screaming. By that time, we were hurrying toward Frasier's door.

It burst open before we could get there. He ran out of the room, saw us, and yelled, "They're gone! They're gone, damn it! She must have stolen them!"

Frasier waved his arms in the air and jumped around like a deranged chimp. His face was purple with rage. As the cops pounded toward us, Will grabbed one of Frasier's arms and said, "Settle down, Michael, or they're going to arrest you for disturbing the peace!"

Frasier stopped yelling and jumping, but he was still breathing like he had just run a mile and looked like he was on the verge of having a stroke.

As the cops came up, one of them warned, "Quiet down, sir, or you'll be in trouble."

"What's the trouble here?" the other one wanted to know.

Frasier took a deep breath and controlled himself with a visible effort. "There are some very valuable papers missing," he said, "and I think Dr. Tamara Paige must have stolen them."

"The manuscript pages from *Cat on a Hot Tin Roof*?" I asked.

He nodded and looked like he was about to cry. "That's right. They're gone."

The words came out of him in a wail of despair. I almost felt sorry for him, but I couldn't quite, because he'd been such a jackass earlier.

One of the cops asked, "If these papers were so valuable, why didn't you put 'em in the safe downstairs?"

"Because no one else knew about them except me and Howard Burleson," Frasier replied.

"The murdered guy?"

"That's right." Frasier glared at Will and me. "At least that was true until tonight. And you can't calculate their worth in money, anyway."

"Still, if they were valuable to you, you shouldn't have left them in your room."

"They were in Howard's room," Frasier said, waving vaguely toward the next door along the corridor. "They were in his suitcase. But we have adjoining rooms, and when I went in there just now to look for them, they were gone."

Both cops frowned at him. One of them said, "You were in the murder victim's room?"

"Well . . . yes." Frasier suddenly looked a little nervous.

"You shouldn't have been," the cop said. "That room should have been sealed off."

"No one told me to stay out of it," Frasier said defensively.

"Ramsey and Nesbit must not have thought about there being an adjoining room," the other cop said. "They're not gonna be happy about this."

"I didn't disturb anything except the suitcase," Frasier said. "I just opened it to look for the papers. I swear I didn't touch anything else this time."

"You were in there earlier?"

"Yes. After Howard and I got back here to the hotel, I went

in there and made sure the door on his side was unlocked, so I could check on him. I didn't want him wandering off again, like he did before."

"But he did wander off," I said. "He went downstairs to the garden where he was killed. Although, technically, they may not have established that yet."

Will said, "I don't see how he could have been killed somewhere else and then lugged through the hotel into that garden."

"You two shouldn't even be discussing that," one of the cops said. "You're civilians."

"Actually, I'm a witness," I said.

"Doesn't matter. This is police business."

"In that case," Frasier said, "I demand that you search Tamara Paige's room. Those pages may still be in there. Maybe she didn't have time to destroy them."

"Why do you think she'd destroy them?"

"Because those pages are my last hope of being able to prove that Howard Burleson wrote *Cat on a Hot Tin Roof*!"

The cops looked confused, and I couldn't blame them. They didn't understand all the hoopla over who wrote what.

Will helped put it in perspective for them by saying, "What Dr. Frasier is talking about could mean that Dr. Paige's career would be ruined."

"Over a stupid play?" one of the cops asked.

"It's not stupid," Frasier said. "It's brilliant. It's just that the wrong man has gotten the credit for that brilliance all these years. Now, are you going to search Dr. Paige's room or not?"

"That's up to Detective Ramsey and Detective Nesbit." The cop who answered took a cell phone from a holder on his belt. "But I'll call them and ask them what they want us to do. In the meantime, Doctor, keep the racket down, okay?"

Frasier sighed and nodded. "All right. But I really need that manuscript before ten o'clock tomorrow morning. That's when my presentation is scheduled. Please make sure the detectives understand that."

The cop nodded. The other officer pointed to the door of Frasier's room and said, "The three of you go in there and wait."

"Hold on a minute," Will said. "Ms. Dickinson and I—"

The cop glared at us and pointed again, this time jabbing the air sharply with his finger. He didn't let Will finish explaining that the two of us didn't have any desire to go into Frasier's room.

It looked like we were going to, though, whether we wanted to or not. Anyway, I'll admit I wanted to be there if the cops searched Tamara's room. Despite my best intentions, I had gotten caught up in the investigation. I wanted to know the truth.

We left the door of Frasier's room open. The bed was rumpled and unmade, but other than that the place was neat. He wasn't the type to throw clothes around a hotel room. The connecting doors between Frasier's room and Howard Burleson's were both open, so I could see into Burleson's room. It was neat, too, except for the suitcase lying open on the bed with its contents strewn around.

The cop stood in the doorway to keep an eye on us and make sure we didn't go into Burleson's room. A couple of minutes later, the other cop came in and said, "I talked to Detective Nesbit. He and Detective Ramsey will be here in about twenty minutes to search that room. Until then, everybody stays out of there, and we're gonna wait right here to make sure of that."

"You don't need Ms. Dickinson and me, then," Will said. He didn't know that I wanted to be there for the search . . . although you would have thought that he knew me well enough by then to guess that I would.

The cop who had called the detectives put out a hand when Will started toward the door. "Nesbit said for everybody to stay put until he and Ramsey get here. That means everybody stays put."

"But we don't have anything to do with this," Will protested.

"I'm just following orders, sir. Why don't you sit down and try to take it easy?"

Will looked like he wanted to argue. I put a hand on his arm and said quietly, "Maybe we'd better do like he says, Will."

He gave me a look that seemed to ask when I'd become so mild-mannered. But then he shrugged and said, "Okay. I still don't see the point in it, though."

There was an uncomfortable twenty minutes while we waited for Ramsey and Nesbit. The cops stood on either side of the doorway. Frasier sat in the chair at the desk, while Will and I took the sofa. My eyes kept straying to the curtains over the French doors, knowing that from the balcony on the other side of those doors, I could have looked down on the scene of Howard Burleson's murder. Then I looked at the connecting doors leading into the old man's room. The fact that the manuscript samples were missing was one more thing that didn't look good for Tamara Paige. I wasn't sure how she could have gotten her hands on them, though.

"Dr. Frasier," I said, "how did Dr. Paige manage to steal that manuscript, if she did? Weren't the doors of both rooms locked?"

"I don't know how she did it," he said, "but I know she's to blame."

"What about the doors?" I persisted.

"Yes, they were locked. At least mine was." Frasier's eyes

widened. "She must have come over here and gotten Howard to open his door. She could have talked him into coming with her and bringing the pages along." He slapped his forehead. "My God! Of course. She suggested they go down to the garden where she could examine the pages while they had a drink. I know how charming she can be . . . when she wants to."

Will said, "And you wouldn't have heard him leaving with her?"

"Not if they left while I was taking a shower. Damn it! I knew I'd have to keep a close eye on Howard while we were here in New Orleans, but I never figured on having to protect him from a murderer!"

I had to admit that Frasier's theory made sense. Everything about it fit, as far as I could see, except for the fact that I didn't want Tamara to be the killer.

Ramsey and Nesbit showed up a short time later. We heard them coming down the hall. Ramsey came in first and glared in surprise at Will and me.

"What are you doing here?"

I nodded toward the two uniformed officers. "Your watchdogs wouldn't let us leave."

"You said for everybody to stay put, Detective," one of the cops said to Nesbit, who had followed Ramsey into the room.

"That's right," Nesbit agreed.

Ramsey frowned at me. "The way you show up around murders all the time, Red, I'm about to start suspecting you."

"Is that right, Red?" I threw right back at him. We were never going to like each other, I thought, and it didn't have anything to do with the color of our hair.

Nesbit started pulling on a pair of latex gloves. "Let's have a look around the victim's room," he suggested. "You two can continue sparring later."

Ramsey didn't look happy with that comment, but he pulled on some gloves, too, and the two detectives stepped carefully through the connecting doors into Howard Burleson's room.

"We would have gotten around to this as soon as we finished questioning Dr. Paige, anyway," Nesbit told us over his shoulder.

"Is she still in custody?" I asked.

"For the time being," Nesbit replied. "She hasn't been charged with anything, though."

Ramsey turned his head and practically snarled at me. "I wanted to charge her with resisting an officer for trying to run like that, but I got overruled."

"I'm the one who tackled her," Nesbit said. "It was my call."

I stood up and moved so that I could see better as they walked into the center of the old man's room and stood there for a couple of minutes, turning slowly and just looking around, taking it all in. Nesbit muttered, "No signs of a struggle."

"What about that suitcase?" Ramsey asked. "Looks like somebody dumped it on the bed, like they were searching for something."

"I did that," Frasier called through the open doors. "I was looking for some papers that Mr. Burleson had with him. They're very important, Detectives. They're part of the reason he was killed!"

Nesbit asked, "Is that why you were in here? Looking for those documents?"

Frasier nodded. "That's right. I didn't touch anything else. But I'll bet if you check, you'll find Tamara Paige's fingerprints in there!"

"We'll cover that base, don't worry," Nesbit said. "Step over to the doorway, Dr. Frasier."

When Frasier had done so, Nesbit went on, "Now, take a look around from there and see if you can tell if anything else is missing."

There wouldn't have been many of the old man's belongings in the room, I thought, except what was in the suitcase. Other than that, it was just a hotel room, albeit a pretty fancy one. Frasier stood in the doorway gazing around for a minute or so, then shook his head.

"Everything looks normal to me," he said. "You won't find anything in here unless it's Dr. Paige's fingerprints, like I told you."

"Don't try to tell us our business," Ramsey said with a glare. "We know what we're doing."

"I'm sorry," Frasier said, but his apology didn't sound too genuine to me. "I'm not trying to tell you what to do, Detective. I just really need to find those pages, if she didn't destroy them. Do you think . . . do you think it would be possible to look in her room?"

Nesbit said, "That's one of the things we were going to do when we got back to the hotel, along with searching this room. I suppose we can go take a look now."

"Can I come with you?" Frasier asked eagerly. "You'll need me to identify the papers, if you find them. And, by all rights, I should have them."

Ramsey shook his head. "Anything we find is evidence. You won't be able to touch it, Doctor."

Frasier looked stricken. He had allowed himself to hope he could still give his presentation, and now that hope had been snatched away from him. He said, "You can't mean that! My career depends on those pages!"

"Sorry, Doctor," Nesbit told him. "Detective Ramsey is right. If those documents are in Dr. Paige's room, they're evidence and will be impounded." He paused. "We might be able to make photocopies of them for you. Would that help?"

Frasier was still upset, but he shrugged a little. "Maybe. At least people could see that the play is in Howard Burleson's handwriting."

I didn't see how that was going to prove anything. Burleson could have sat down and copied Tennessee Williams's play out of a book. But the pages would be something, anyway, for Frasier to present at the festival in support of his theory, even if they didn't prove it. They would show that Burleson hadn't been lying about having a handwritten manuscript of the play.

"All right, come along, Doctor," Nesbit said as he and Ramsey came back into Frasier's room and headed for the door.

Will and I were on our feet. "What about us?" I asked.

"What about you?" Ramsey asked. "This is none of your business."

"Actually," Will said, "I could help Dr. Frasier identify any manuscript pages you find, if you find any. I'm quite familiar with Tennessee Williams's work and have published several articles about it."

I wondered if he was saying this just so I could tag along and observe the investigation. Maybe he had realized by now that my curiosity was up.

I added, "And since I feel a certain responsibility to my clients, I'd like to go along to see that Dr. Paige's interests are protected."

Ramsey gave me a withering stare. "You're not an attorney, and, anyway, we're not going to do anything illegal."

"Do you have a search warrant for her room?"

"As a matter of fact, we do," Ramsey said with a smirk. "But you know what? You can come with us. I know what you want to do."

"You do?"

"Yeah. You want to play detective, just like you did those other times. You think you're gonna figure out the case and show up the dumb cops."

"I never said that," I insisted.

But there was a smattering of truth in what he said. Not about me thinking they were dumb, of course. I didn't like Ramsey, but I had no idea how smart he was . . . or wasn't. I just wanted to see if there was any other explanation for the growing evidence that pointed toward Tamara.

Nesbit smiled slightly and said, "Personally, I think it might be better to have Ms. Dickinson where we can keep an eye on her. That way we'll know she's not doing anything to hinder the investigation."

"Thanks . . . I think," I said.

Ramsey made a curt gesture for me, Will, and Frasier to follow them, then left the room with Nesbit. Ramsey told the two uniformed cops to stay there and keep the scene secure. He used a walkie-talkie to call downstairs and tell the forensics team to come up and go over Howard Burleson's room when they were finished with the crime scene in the garden.

We went down the hall and stopped in front of a doorway. Ramsey and Nesbit seemed to know that this was Tamara's room. I realized they must have gotten that information from Dale Gillette.

That wasn't all they had gotten. Nesbit took a key card from his pocket and used it to unlock the door. He was still wearing the latex gloves, so he grasped the handle, turned it, and swung the door open. He looked back at the three of us civilians and said, "Stay in the hall. Don't even step inside the door."

We nodded. The two detectives went in. Will and Frasier and I crowded up close so that we could look into the room and watch as Ramsey and Nesbit walked around looking at everything.

I felt bad for Tamara, having a couple of strangers pawing through her stuff. A woman needs some privacy, even for her possessions.

There wasn't really much to see in the room, though. Tamara had hung her clothes in the closet, but her under-things were still in her suitcase. I figured her makeup kit and things like that would be in the bathroom.

Her laptop was open on the writing table, with a slide show of photographs serving as her screensaver. I could see them from where I stood. Most of them seemed to be family pho-tos—of a bunch of people I didn't know, of course—but there were also a few landscape shots and some pictures of dogs and cats. A paperback book lay on the table next to the computer. I could see enough of its cover to recognize it as a copy of *Cat on a Hot Tin Roof*. She had probably been looking through it earlier while she was thinking about Howard Burleson's story, before she started working out.

Nesbit said, "I don't see any handwritten papers, Dr. Frasier. You did say they were handwritten, didn't you?"

"That's right," Frasier said. "Mr. Burleson wrote the play in a legal pad, so the samples would be on lined yellow paper of that size."

"Nothing like that in here." Nesbit picked up Tamara's lap-top case, which was sitting on the floor next to the table, and looked in it. "Nothing here, either."

A look of sweaty desperation appeared on Frasier's face. He could see his last hopes slipping away. "Keep looking," he said. "Please."

Ramsey gestured toward the open door that led into the bathroom. "I'll check in there." Nesbit nodded.

I didn't think it was very likely that Tamara would have

hidden the pages in the bathroom—if she had taken them, that is—but I supposed anything was possible.

Ramsey had been inside the bathroom only a moment when he said, "Hello."

Nesbit hurried over there. "What is it?"

"Looks like a little bit of ash around the drain in the sink."

"Ash?" Frasier repeated. At that moment, his face was about the same color as ashes.

Nesbit said, "Yes, it looks like something's been burned in here, and then the ashes were washed down the drain except for a few tiny pieces. Wait a minute, maybe I can get one of them . . ."

Frasier looked like he was about to burst into tears. His hands knotted together. I thought for a second he was going to pray, then decided that he just wasn't the type. Then he started murmuring something and for a second I thought I was wrong, that he was praying after all.

Then I realized that he was saying, "Shit, shit, shit," over and over again.

Nesbit emerged from the bathroom with a pair of needle-nose tweezers in one hand and a clear plastic evidence bag in the other. He held up the bag and said, "Take a look at that, Dr. Frasier."

At first glance, I thought the bag was empty. Then I spotted the tiny piece of burned paper inside it, a ragged square about a quarter of an inch on each side. Most of it was gray ash, but along one side a strip of unburned paper remained.

It was yellow, just like the paper from a legal pad.

"She burned them," Frasier whispered. He lifted his hands to his temples. "She burned them."

And then he really did start to cry. Tears rolled down his cheeks as he clutched at his hair.

Nesbit said quietly, "For the record, Dr. Frasier, do you recognize that paper?"

Frasier jerked his head up and down.

"That's it, then," Ramsey said with a note of finality in his voice. "We'll seal this room, and then we'd better get back."

And even though he didn't say it, we all knew what they were going back to do.

They were going to arrest Dr. Tamara Paige and charge her with the murder of Howard Burleson.

Chapter 14

Ramsey and Nesbit didn't tell us that, of course. Far be it from them to let us in on what they were planning, especially Ramsey.

But it was obvious, and even though I didn't like it, there was nothing I could do about it. Anyway, judging by everything I had seen tonight, there was a good chance Tamara was guilty, and I disliked one of my clients killing another of my clients even more.

The detectives told us to go back to our rooms and keep ourselves available for further questioning. A distraught Michael Frasier stumbled off to his room. Will walked with me back to mine, and we paused in the doorway before I went in.

"You know Dr. Paige a lot better than I do, Will," I said to him. "Do you really think she could have done such a thing?"

Will thought it over for a long moment before he shrugged. "Before tonight, I would have said no, not in a million years. Tamara and I aren't close, but I've known her for years, and I've never seen any signs that she has a violent nature."

"A lot of people don't . . . until they're pushed too far."

He nodded. "That's true. And I know that she's very dedicated to her work. She's not married, doesn't have any close family . . ." He shrugged again. "So her work means a lot to her. What bothers me is that she didn't seem the least bit convinced that Howard Burleson was telling the truth. It seems a lot more likely to me that she would have just let Frasier go on with his presentation, because she believed that Burleson's claims would be discredited."

I thought about what he'd said, then told him, "You're right, unless something happened to change her mind."

"Like what?"

I started putting things together in my mind. "Maybe Frasier's right about how Dr. Paige got her hands on those manuscript samples. Maybe she went to Burleson's room and convinced the old man to show them to her. She could have decided to check them out for herself, before Frasier's presentation. And you saw how Burleson was. I think she could have talked him into showing her the pages without much trouble."

"Yeah, that's probably true," Will said.

Warming up to the speculation, I went on. "I don't think she intended to hurt the old man when she went to his room. She just wanted to look at the pages and confirm that he was either delusional or lying to get the attention. But if she saw something in the manuscript that convinced her he was telling the truth . . ."

"She could have decided that she couldn't risk letting Frasier go on with his presentation," Will concluded.

I nodded. "Yeah. So she talks Burleson into going downstairs with her, takes him out into the garden so they can talk some more, she tells him, and then once they're out of sight of everybody . . ."

I couldn't make myself go on, and this time Will didn't finish my thought. He just nodded and looked grim.

"There's only one thing wrong with that theory," I said after a moment.

"What?"

"I can't believe that she's a murderer."

"Nobody else would have had a motive to kill that harmless old man," Will said. "And I don't like thinking that about Tamara any more than you do."

"Nobody else that we *know of*. But maybe something else is going on, something we don't even know about."

Actually, I was thinking that I might know about it. I couldn't shake the memories of the two times I'd seen Callie Madison earlier tonight, first on the balcony of Dr. Jeffords's room, then hurrying through the hotel garden right after I'd found Burleson's body. Thinking that Callie might have killed the old man because he had seen her returning from her rendezvous with Jeffords was mighty farfetched ... but was it any more farfetched than Callie fooling around with Jeffords in the first place?

There was Dr. Ian Keller to consider, too. He had been in the garden before I'd found the body. Probably perfectly innocently, of course. Hotel guests probably cut through there all the time. But I figured it was still worth talking to Keller and trying to find out exactly what he'd been doing there.

Those were just two possibilities off the top of my head. There could be others that, like I'd told Will, we weren't even aware of.

The problem was that Ramsey and Nesbit weren't going to do any more real investigating. They had their suspect under arrest, and from here on out they would only be looking for evidence that would support the charges against Tamara. They probably wouldn't even consider any other theory, let alone look into one.

So that left it up to somebody else.

"Delilah," Will said slowly, "I've seen that look on your

face before. You know how upset those detectives will be if you interfere with their investigation."

"What investigation?" I asked. "They're convinced that Tamara did it. The investigation is over." I paused. "It's a prosecution now."

I could see in his eyes that he knew I was right. He was worried anyway, of course. I didn't blame him. I didn't like the idea of poking around and trying to uncover a killer, either.

But unless Tamara confessed—which was still a possibility— I wasn't going to be convinced she was guilty, evidence or no evidence. A little scrap of half-burned paper wasn't conclusive. Not for me, anyway.

"Just be careful," Will said. "The festival will go on, despite what's happened, and I'm going to be pretty busy for the next few days. I won't be able to stay with you all the time and help you."

My temper flared a little. "You mean you won't be able to protect me."

He shrugged but didn't deny what I'd said.

"Listen here, Will Burke," I said. "I can take care of myself. And it's not like you're John Wayne—you're an English professor."

As soon as I said that, I wished I hadn't. It was hurtful and I knew it. But I couldn't call the words back.

Will just smiled faintly and shook his head. "No, I'm not, am I?" he said.

"Will, I'm sorry. I didn't mean—"

He held up a hand to stop me. "No, no, you're absolutely right, Delilah. Look, I just don't want you to get hurt, so like I said, please be careful."

"I will," I promised.

"And if there is anything I can do to help you, please let me know."

"Sure." I put a hand behind his neck and came up on my toes to kiss him. "I'm sorry, Will . . ." I murmured.

"It's all right. Really." He kissed me then, and if it hadn't been so late . . . if I hadn't stumbled over a corpse earlier in the night . . . if I hadn't said such a dumb thing . . .

Well, *if, if, if,* you know how that goes. Sometimes I think *if* is one of the most useless words in the English language, because most of the time it's just pointing out where you went wrong and there's not a blasted thing you can do to change it. You can't go back. All you can do is keep going forward and hope for the best.

Life can be a bitch that way.

I didn't sleep well that night. I was haunted by half-waking dreams of Howard Burleson's bloody, lifeless face, and when I finally did fall sound asleep, I found myself in the middle of the movie version of *Cat on a Hot Tin Roof* . . . and no matter how broodingly handsome Paul Newman was, it wasn't a pleasant experience. All the emotional turmoil swirled around me like floodwaters and nearly pulled me down. I woke up gasping as if I'd really been drowning.

After that I dozed some more but never really did go back to sleep, so I was tired and cranky when I got up the next morning. A shower helped a little, and I hoped some hot coffee would help even more. It was a little after seven o'clock when I left the room and headed for the elevators, intending to avail myself of the breakfast buffet that was planned for the hotel's ballroom that morning.

I got in the elevator alone and the doors were sliding shut when I heard someone call, "Hold that elevator, please!" Without thinking, I pushed the DOORS OPEN button, and they slid back.

Callie Madison stood there, a little breathless.

She gave me a bright smile and said, "Ms. Dickinson! Good morning. How are you today?"

She was so chipper and cheerful I thought to myself that she couldn't possibly have heard about Howard Burleson's murder or Tamara's arrest. I also thought that Dr. Jeffords must be a lot more of a tiger in bed than he looked, if Callie was still this perky the next morning.

But what I said, without answering her question, was, "Are you goin' down to breakfast?"

"That's right." Callie stepped into the elevator and pushed the button for the ground floor.

"How was your evening?" I asked. "Is your husband enjoyin' New Orleans?"

"Oh, as much as Jake can enjoy any vacation, I suppose," she replied with a little laugh. "After the opening ceremonies last night, we went to Paul Prudhomme's and he ate like he usually does . . . like a bear about to go into hibernation. But he seemed to have a good time."

"When I eat a big meal like that, it usually puts me right to sleep."

She laughed again. "Jake's the same way. I swear, he was sound asleep ten minutes after we got back to the hotel, and an earthquake couldn't have budged him. Except they don't have earthquakes here, do they? They have hurricanes. All right, a hurricane couldn't have budged him." She sobered as the indicator light on the panel above the door changed from the second floor to the first. We were almost to the lobby. "Oh, that was in bad taste, wasn't it? I shouldn't bring up hurricanes after what happened here a few years ago."

"They're still a fact of life," I pointed out. "Folks here can't ignore 'em."

"I suppose that's true."

The elevator came to a stop. I had found out a little that I wanted to know, but there was still more. As we stepped out, I went on. "What did you do the rest of the evening, if your husband turned in early?"

"Actually, I relished the opportunity to take a long hot bath and read some."

She told the lie with conviction and, at this point, I wasn't going to challenge her on it. Instead, as we started walking toward the ballroom, I asked her, "What's Mr. Madison going to do today while you're at the conference? Or is he going to attend, too?"

"Jake?" She smiled and shook her head. "Jake's not interested in such things. He's going to do some sightseeing. He owns a construction company, so he always has to check out the buildings everywhere he goes and see what methods other people in the business are using."

"Well, I hope he has a good time."

"I'm sure he will. And then tonight we're going to hit some jazz clubs."

We walked into the ballroom, and I noticed right away how somber the mood was. The news of the old man's murder and Tamara's arrest must be getting around, I thought. And as the eyes of the professors swung toward me and stared with morbid curiosity, I knew they'd heard about my part in the discovery of the body, too.

"My, everyone certainly looks serious this morning," Callie commented. "Who died?"

I knew she wasn't serious—either that, or she knew more than she let on and was pretending ignorance—but I answered her anyway. "Howard Burleson," I said.

She looked at me and started to frown. "What? Wait . . . you mean somebody really died? Who did you say?"

"Howard Burleson."

"That old man Michael Frasier brought along?"

"That's right."

"My God!" Callie pressed a hand to her chest. "That's awful! What happened? Did he have a heart attack?"

That seemed to be everybody's first reaction to the news that Burleson was dead. With somebody that old, it wasn't an unreasonable assumption. On the other hand, somebody who was mixed up in Burleson's murder would probably pretend to react the same way, just to keep suspicion from falling on them.

"No, he didn't have a heart attack," I said. "He was murdered."

Callie's eyes widened even more. "Murdered?" she repeated in a hushed voice. "Are you sure?"

"Pretty darned sure. I was the one who found the body in the garden, there in the atrium, so I saw the blood and how his head was bashed in."

She was pretty fair skinned to start with, and she turned even paler when she heard that. "In the . . . the atrium?" she said.

"Yeah. Right there in the middle of all those plants."

"When?"

I shook my head. "I'm not sure exactly when he was killed, but the police have probably narrowed down the time of death by now. But it was between midnight and one when June Powers and I found the body."

"June? What's she got to do with this?"

"We were looking for her father-in-law. He'd slipped off to the garden and was gettin' drunk."

"Larry Powers was out there, too?"

"That's right."

I saw the nervousness in her eyes. Obviously the garden had had more occupants last night than she had thought would be there when she cut across it. Whether she was nervous because she was feeling guilty about her affair with Jeffords, or because she was afraid somebody might have seen her kill Burleson, I didn't know.

I went on, "I'm surprised you hadn't heard all about this. The police were going to question everybody in the hotel."

She shook her head. "No one told me about it. No one came to our room. I haven't talked to the police."

Once I thought about that for a second, I wasn't surprised. Ramsey and Nesbit had planned to canvass the whole hotel, but once they arrested Tamara Paige, I suppose they had decided the questioning no longer had the same urgency. They had probably called it off and would be back today to finish up, rather than disturbing everybody in the middle of the night.

"Have they arrested anyone yet?" Callie asked.

"I don't know," I answered, and it wasn't exactly a lie. Even though I felt sure Tamara had been charged with the murder by now and would probably be arraigned this morning, I didn't actually know that. Nobody had told me one way or the other.

A little shiver went through her. "I hope they catch whoever did it soon."

"You and me both."

"I'm sorry about Mr. Burleson," Callie continued. "He seemed like a nice, friendly old man. A real Southern gentleman."

I nodded. "He was that, no doubt about it."

"Do you believe he really knew Tennessee Williams?" She didn't know anything about Burleson's claim to have written *Cat on a Hot Tin Roof* . . . or at least was pretending not to know anything about it.

"They might have been acquainted," I said. "We may

never know. What's your interest in Williams? Do you special-ize in his work like some of the others who come to the festi-val?"

I didn't mention Tamara by name.

Callie shook her head. "No, not really. I've taught his work in some of my classes, of course, but my interest is more in Southern literature in general. Faulkner, Flannery O'Connor, Lansdale, *Gone With the Wind, To Kill a Mockingbird* . . . things like that." She paused. "This is really going to cast a shadow over the festival, isn't it?"

"I imagine so."

"And poor Dr. Frasier must be devastated, since Mr. Burleson was his friend."

I didn't bother to correct that impression, although I knew that Frasier hadn't been the old man's friend. Burleson was just a means to an end for Frasier, a way to further his career and damage Tamara Paige's at the same time.

"But I suppose life goes on," Callie said with a sigh. "I'm going to get some coffee and something to eat. I have a panel later this morning, and I'll need to get ready for it after break-fast."

"All right. I'll see you later."

Callie gave me a nod and headed for the buffet table. I hes-itated, looking around the room to see if Will was here yet. For the most part, people had stopped looking at me and gone back to eating, but I caught a few of them still sneaking glances at me. I guess finding corpses is bound to give a per-son a certain amount of notoriety.

I didn't see Will anywhere, but I did spot June, Edgar, and Larry Powers sitting at one of the round tables. I fixed myself a cup of coffee and then strolled over to the table. I wanted to find out how Larry was doing this morning, after his binge the night before. He didn't look too happy. He was scowling down into a coffee cup with a plate of apparently untouched food in front of him.

"Mornin', folks," I greeted the three of them as I came up to the table. I put my free hand on Larry's shoulder. "Dr. Powers, how are you feelin' today?"

"Like every venomous serpent in the world crawled down my throat, curled up in my guts, and died," he rumbled without looking up.

"Ooookay," I said. "A mite hungover, are you?"

"More than a mite. But if you were inquiring about my medical condition—"

"He's fine," June broke in. "I've already talked to his oncologist and his gastroenterologist this morning. They were extremely upset about what happened, but agreed that in the absence of new symptoms, Papa Larry probably didn't do any new damage to himself." She glared at him. "Not for lack of trying, though."

Edgar asked, "Have they found out any more about that old man's murder?"

I dodged the question, as I had with Callie. "I don't really know. I haven't heard anything new this morning."

"It's a terrible thing, just terrible." Edgar sounded sincere. June seemed to think he didn't have any emotions, but I wasn't sure about that. I figured it was more a matter of the two of them just not connecting anymore. I knew from painful personal experience how that sometimes happened.

Despite the bad night I'd had, I was actually hungry this morning, so I said, "I'll see you folks later. I think I'll get something to eat."

"The bacon is excellent," Edgar said.

Larry groaned. With his hangover, I wasn't surprised that the idea of eating didn't appeal to him right now.

As I went to the buffet table, I noticed that Callie had filled a plate, gotten some coffee, and gone over to sit with some of the other professors. Dr. Jeffords was at the same table, but he was several chairs away from Callie and didn't seem to be paying any particular attention to her. She was acting the same way toward him. I wondered just how much practice they'd had at covering up their affair. It could be something new, or it could have been going on for some time. Without coming right out and asking her, I wouldn't know, and I wasn't ready to do that just yet.

I started filling a plate with biscuits, gravy, scrambled eggs, and bacon. The food looked and smelled good. Callie was right about one thing: in spite of death and murder, life went on for those of us who were still here. I was looking forward to digging in and satisfying my appetite.

It looked like that might have to wait awhile, though, because as I neared the end of the buffet table, a heavy hand suddenly fell on my shoulder.

CHAPTER 15

I managed to control my reaction so that I didn't drop my food and coffee, but the man whose hand was on my shoulder must have felt me jump a little. As I turned, I half expected to see Detective Ramsey or Detective Nesbit—the grip felt like that of a cop—but instead I saw the gruff but worried face of Dr. Ian Keller.

"I'm sorry, Ms. Dickinson," he said. "I didn't mean to startle you."

"That's all right," I told him.

"I just wanted to say that I heard about what happened last night, and I'm sorry."

"About Mr. Burleson, you mean?"

"Yeah, that, too, but mainly about you finding the body like that. I know how upsetting a thing like that can be."

The way he phrased that made me wonder. He hadn't said that he could *guess* how upsetting it was to stumble over a corpse. He said he *knew*. I had to ask myself if he was speaking from personal experience.

But all I said was, "Thank you. It was a bad night, all right."

"I'm sure." He turned his head to look out over the ballroom. "There's an empty table over there. Would you mind if we had breakfast together?"

I couldn't figure out why he wanted to sit with me while we ate, but since I wanted to talk to him anyway, I wasn't going to refuse. I said, "Nope, that'll be fine."

He smiled. "Good. I'll get my food and join you in just a minute."

I went over to the table Keller had indicated, and, true to his word, he sat down next to me as soon as he had filled his plate. And I do mean filled. It was heaped high with pancakes, eggs, sausage, and slices of ham. He had managed to juggle a cup of coffee and a glass of orange juice, too. It was a lot of food, but he was a big guy. It probably took a lot to keep him going.

I was curious why he wanted to have breakfast with me, so I asked him about it, indirectly. "I'm surprised you didn't want to eat with some of your colleagues."

He shook his head. "Nah. Other than the academic stuff, we don't have a lot in common. And I get enough of that at the university."

"I'm not sure what the two of us have in common. You said you're from New Jersey, and I was born and raised in Georgia."

He grinned. "Jaw-ja. I love that accent."

I could have been offended, but I just lowered my voice and said, "Yeah, ya don't hear dem guys up in Joisey talkin' like dat, do ya?"

Keller laughed and slapped the table lightly beside his plate. "You see, that's what I'm talkin' about. You're down to earth, Ms. Dickinson. You have a sense of humor. You don't take everything so seriously all the time. Like me."

"Well, I don't sit around broodin', if that's what you mean."

"Yeah. There's enough crappy stuff in life that if you tried to figure out all of it, you'd never have time to do anything else."

Even though he still had a smile on his face as he said that, I saw something flicker through his eyes. Something like pain, or regret. I wondered what had caused it. I had a feeling he wouldn't appreciate me asking about it, though.

He changed the subject by asking, "Have the reporters been bothering you this morning?"

"No. I didn't know there were any around." I wasn't surprised, though, considering what had happened.

"Oh, they're out there, nosing around about the murder. You must've gotten lucky when you came down from your room. You made it in here without any of them spotting you. Just a heads-up, they're probably gonna be lurking in the lobby when you go out."

"Thanks for the warning," I said with a nod. "It's not gonna do them any good. All I can say is 'no comment.' "

Keller grunted. "Yeah, the cops wouldn't like it if you started spoutin' off about the case. They can't really stop you if you want to talk to the reporters, but they can give you a hard time about it. And you don't wanna be on their bad side."

He sounded like a man who'd been given a hard time by the cops in the past, but maybe I was just stereotyping him because he looked a little like a movie mobster, I told myself. I didn't want to be guilty of judging anybody by appearances.

We devoted ourselves to the food for a few minutes. It was good, especially when it was washed down by the excellent coffee. I was still tired, but I was starting to feel better.

When Dr. Keller spoke up again, he said, "So, it was out there in that garden you found the old man, eh?"

"That's right," I said with a slight frown. The fact that he had asked the question took me a little by surprise. Earlier, he had seemed like he really didn't want to talk about the murder.

But maybe that was just to put me off my guard, I thought.

Was it possible that now he was trying to pump me about what had happened and what I might have seen?

"Who would've thought that such an ugly thing could happen in such a pretty place?"

"You've been out there?"

"Yeah, I cut across there yesterday evening to get back to my room," he answered without hesitation. "I thought it might save some time. It really didn't, though. Those paths twist and turn so much, you could probably walk around the garden faster than you can walk through it."

That was true. And the way he had admitted so readily that he'd been there ought to be an indication that he didn't have anything to hide, I thought. I couldn't really bring myself to accept that fully, though, at least not yet.

"Have the police questioned you yet?" I asked him.

He frowned. "Why would they want to question me?"

"Well, they said they were going to canvass everybody in the hotel, just to find out if anybody saw anything that might have a bearing on the case. And since you were actually in the garden last night . . ."

"Yeah, but that was a good while before the murder—wait a minute." He put his fork down, his eyes narrowing as he stared at me. His jovial manner disappeared in an instant. "You're questioning me right now, aren't you? I've been interrogated before, lady, and I know a grilling when I hear it!"

The anger I saw on his big, beefy face made me a little nervous, but I didn't think he was going to do anything in a ballroom full of witnesses. "You just said you were out there before the murder took place. How do you know—"

"How do I know when the murder took place if I'm not the killer?" He grunted and shook his head. "Yeah, that's the way people think, all right. Always in a hurry to jump to conclusions. Makin' something out of some innocent comment, or who you're related to."

I hadn't said anything about who he was related to. I didn't know anything about any of his relatives.

But before I could point that out, he went on. "Listen, I don't know when the old man was killed. He may have been lyin' there dead when I cut through the garden, for all I know. But I heard it was after midnight when you found him, and I know it was before that when I was in the garden. That's all I meant. Maybe I didn't phrase it as clearly as I could have, but don't go making that out to mean that I'm a murderer."

As upset as he already was, I didn't think this was a very good time to mention that I had known all along he was in the garden because I'd seen him there. He would have taken that as more evidence that I was grilling him, as he'd put it.

Which, of course, I was.

"I'm sorry," I said. "I didn't mean to offend you, Dr. Keller. It just struck me as strange when you said that, and I wanted to be sure I understood."

"You got it clear now?"

I nodded. "Yes, I think so."

"Good."

What was really clear was that I was even more suspicious of him now than I had been starting out . . . but I wasn't about to tell him that.

After a moment, he said, "I'm sorry, too. I didn't mean to bark at you, Ms. Dickinson. It's just that I've had people make snap judgments about me before, so that's sort of a pet peeve of mine."

"I understand," I said again.

At the same time, I spotted Will coming into the ballroom. I was glad to see him. For one thing, I still felt a little bad about what I'd said the night before. For another, he did look a little like John Wayne to me—metaphorically speaking, anyway—as he started across the room toward the table where Dr. Keller and I were sitting. I would be glad for Will's company once he got here.

Then two more men came into the ballroom just a few steps behind Will, and I wasn't as happy to see them. Detectives Ramsey and Nesbit stopped just inside the room and looked around. Ramsey was wearing sunglasses. He reached up and took them off in a move that looked practiced to me, like he had stood in front of a mirror and worked on his hard-boiled cop attitude.

The people who were eating breakfast slowly took notice of the two newcomers and the place got quiet again. Ramsey and Nesbit looked past Will, spotted me at the table, and started toward me. Almost every eye in the room followed them. English professors are just as much voyeurs as anybody else. Maybe more so because they can see the inherent drama in any situation.

Will reached the table. In a low, hurried voice, he said, "Here come those two detectives."

"I see 'em," I said with resignation in my voice. "I knew I'd probably have to deal with them again today—"

"They're not looking for you." Will's gaze swung over to Keller. "I overheard them talking to Gillette in the lobby. It's you they want to talk to, Ian."

That surprised me. When I was talking to Ramsey and Nesbit the night before, I had mentioned seeing Keller in the garden, but once they settled on Tarama as their leading suspect, I'd figured they would forget about him.

I didn't have time to mull it over. The two detectives came up to the table and Ramsey said, "Dr. Ian Keller?"

"Yeah," Keller said, and his tone was harder and flatter than I had ever heard it.

"From New Jersey?" Nesbit asked.

"I live in Atlanta."

Ramsey said, "But you're from New Jersey. Don't try BSing us, Keller. We know who you are. We got your mug shots from the cops in Newark and surveillance photos from the FBI's RICO task force."

I tried not to stare. Mug shots? The FBI? RICO? Wasn't that some sort of organized crime thing?

Keller didn't look happy about being confronted like this, but he didn't seem too fazed by it. He took his napkin from his lap, folded it neatly, and set it beside his still half-full plate.

"If you have all of that, then you know that all the indictments against me were dropped," he said. "My name was cleared. I was never put on trial for anything." He paused. "Besides, that was twenty years ago, when I was just a young man."

Ramsey had that annoying smirk on his face again. "Yeah, twenty years ago," he said. "Twenty-five to life, that was the sentence your brother got, wasn't it? So he's still behind bars, isn't he, just like you would be if you didn't have a brother who loved you enough to take the fall for you."

Keller slowly shook his head. "Terry committed those crimes, not me. He confessed, and there was plenty of evidence to back up his confession." He looked over at Nesbit. "You must know all this, even if Dirty Harry there doesn't want to admit it."

Ramsey's smirk turned into a snarl. Nesbit put a hand out toward him and said to Keller, "We'd just like to ask you a few questions, Doctor. We'll be talking to all the members of your group about what happened to Howard Burleson. I'm sure you've heard about it."

"Yeah. But I don't know a thing that could help you."

"You'd better let us be the judge of that."

"Yeah, because cops never make a mistake, do they?"

Ramsey still looked mad, and Nesbit was beginning to get annoyed, too. "Please come with us, Dr. Keller," he said. "The hotel management has been kind enough to provide us with a room where we can conduct our interviews."

I was sure Dale Gillette would have provided whatever the cops wanted if he thought it would get the case cleared up sooner and minimize the bad publicity for the St. Emilion.

Keller sighed and then scraped his chair back. He managed to smile at me as he stood up. "I'm sorry we didn't get to finish our breakfast together, Ms. Dickinson, and I regret that little misunderstanding earlier, too. But perhaps now you can see why I'm a little sensitive on the subject."

"What's he talking about?" Ramsey asked.

"Nothing," Keller said as he came around the table. "A personal matter."

"I wasn't asking you, Keller."

"Dr. Keller."

"Yeah? What'd you major in, leg breaking?"

The whole ballroom was still and quiet now as everybody looked on. At that moment, I felt sorry for Keller. I didn't know what he had done in the past . . . I wasn't even sure that he hadn't killed Howard Burleson . . . but I still thought Ramsey was being a jerk. And Nesbit was going along with it. It was entirely possible that Keller hadn't had anything at all to do with Burleson's murder, but they were embarrassing him in front of several dozen of his colleagues anyway, after he had obviously gone to a lot of trouble to build a new life for himself.

"Let's just get this over with," he said. He looked around the room and raised his voice as he added, "Sorry for the interruption, folks. Just go on with your breakfast. I'll see you later at the conference."

"Maybe," Ramsey said. He definitely made the word sound ominous.

The three of them left, and as soon as the ballroom doors swung closed behind them, the noise of startled conversations welled up. I contributed to it myself by leaning toward Will and asking, "What do you think he did?"

"You mean, to get in trouble with the law years ago?" He shook his head. "I have no idea."

"I'll bet we can find out," I said as I pushed my chair back. Like Keller, I had only eaten about half my breakfast, but I wasn't really hungry anymore. I was too curious for that.

I knew I was jumping to conclusions, just like Keller had accused me of, and I also knew that if he turned out to be guilty, it wouldn't be any better for my agency than it would be if Tamara was the killer. Both of them were my clients, part of the group I had brought here to New Orleans. But on a purely instinctive, selfish level, I liked Tamara more than I did Keller, and I could see him being a murderer a lot more easily than I could her.

"Wait a minute," Will said. "I haven't eaten anything yet."

"Well, grab a cup of coffee and a bagel and bring it with you," I told him. "Of course, you don't have to come with me . . ."

"No, that's all right, I'm coming. I guess being around you as much as I have, that curiosity of yours is rubbing off on me."

A few minutes later, we were in the elevator riding up to the third floor. When we got to my room, I sat down at the desk, opened my laptop, and plugged into the high-speed Internet connection. It took only a moment to run a search for Ian Keller, New Jersey, and organized crime.

More than a thousand hits popped up.

Will leaned in to read over my shoulder. "Most of those pages look like they're from newspaper archives," he said.

"Yeah, mostly the Newark paper," I said as I scanned over the list on the screen. "But there are pages from the *New York Times* and other New York papers, too. Must've been a pretty big story. I don't remember ever hearing about it, though."

"Yeah, well, it was in New Jersey," Will pointed out. "And look at the dates. How much attention would you have paid back then to something about organized crime in New Jersey?"

"None at all," I admitted. "I had a newborn baby, so all I was thinking about was diapers and crying and feeling like I'd never be allowed to sleep again."

"Why don't you click on one of those links, and we'll see just what it was Dr. Keller's supposed to have done?"

I followed Will's suggestion and clicked on the first link. It led to a lengthy article about a racketeering investigation carried out by the Newark police in conjunction with the FBI.

And it wasn't a pretty story.

The focus of the investigation was the city's garbage collection contractor. One of the executives of the company that operated the garbage trucks was a man named Terrence Keller. Terrence Keller and his younger brother Ian were reputed to have mob ties and also to be connected with the IRA and other shady factions. According to the story, the cops and the feds had come up with a couple of witnesses willing to testify that the garbage company had used blackmail, extortion, and intimidation to secure the contract with the city, and that the man in charge of that part of the operation was Terrence Keller. Not only that, but Ian Keller was supposedly the actual muscle of the outfit and had terrorized a couple of city officials into going along with the deal by threatening their families.

That didn't sound at all like the sort of man who would wind up with a doctorate in English and write scholarly books and articles about Southern authors.

It got worse, though. The two witnesses, a pair of brothers who had worked for the garbage collection company at one time, had disappeared before they could ever testify before the grand jury, and several days later their bodies had been found at a landfill. They had been chopped into pieces, so identifying them was sort of like putting together the pieces of a jigsaw puzzle, according to the lurid, breathless reporting in the newspaper. The cops found somebody who had seen Ian Keller in the building where the brothers lived, about the time of the murder. He'd been arrested and charged with killing them.

Even I knew that was pretty flimsy evidence, strictly a circumstantial case. But men had been convicted on less. When Ian Keller's fingerprints were found in the brothers' apartment, the case got even stronger.

But then Terrence Keller had confessed to the killings. He claimed that Ian hadn't had anything to do with the murders or the corruption that had led to the RICO investigation. It was true that Ian had gone to the brothers' building that night, but only because he was following his own brother in the hope of preventing Terrence from killing the two witnesses. According to Terrence's story, Ian had been trying to convince him to get out of the mob for a long time.

The cops had originally been inclined not to believe Terrence. They thought he was just trying to shield his younger brother. But Terrence had provided details that only the killer would have known (the newspaper article didn't go into specifics, but I imagined they were pretty gruesome), and had led the cops to the place he had hidden the blood-soaked clothes he'd been wearing on the night of the killings. That blood matched the blood types of the murdered men. Faced with that evidence, along with Terrence's confession, the district attorney had dropped the charges against Ian and the cops had arrested Terrence. He was convicted and sent to prison.

I quickly checked some follow-up stories and found that Ian Keller had dropped out of sight after that, and the speculation was that he had left town.

That turned out to be true, and Will and I knew where he had gone. He had moved south, gone to college, and made a completely different life for himself than the one he had seemed destined to lead. He had reinvented himself, as the old saying goes. He hadn't changed his name, which indicated that he wasn't really trying to hide out or keep anybody from finding out who he was, but the chances of anybody connecting a doctoral student—and then a professor—in Georgia with a reputed gangland killer in New Jersey were pretty slim, same name or not.

"Wow," Will said when he finished reading over my shoulder.

"Yeah," I agreed. "Wow."

"I never would have dreamed . . . I mean, sure, Ian's a big, tough-looking guy. But I thought maybe he had started out as one of those—what did they used to call them?—blue-collar intellectuals. You know, like a dockworker or a truck driver who reads all the time. I never expected him to turn out to be a gangster, even though he looked like one."

I pointed to the screen. "This says he was cleared of all charges. That was the only time he was ever arrested, and the case never went to trial. There's no proof he was ever even in the mob."

"Maybe he wasn't. Maybe he and his brother were both telling the truth."

"Even so, wouldn't all this have turned up when the university ran a background check on him before they hired him?" I asked.

"You'd think so. You're wondering why they gave him a position if they knew all about this?"

"Well . . . yeah."

"The charges were dropped," Will said with a shrug. "In the eyes of the law, he's an innocent man. They had no reason not to hire him."

"What about fear of lawsuits if it came out they had a guy teaching kids who'd been accused of chopping up two other guys?"

"It's not quite the same thing when you're talking about college students. Sure, some of them have parents who are really protective of them, but they're all adults, legally, anyway. And if they had refused to hire Ian when all his credentials were in order, he might have turned around and filed some sort of discrimination suit against them. I'm not saying he would have won, mind you—I don't think he would have—but the administration wouldn't have wanted the hassle of a lawsuit, anyway." Will shook his head. "Here's what it comes down to. Ian Keller is highly respected for his academic achievements and there's never been a hint of scandal or trouble attached to his name while he's been at the university, at least as far as I know. He's well liked and one of the top people in the department."

"He may not be after word of this gets around," I said.

"All anybody knows is that the police came to talk to him. I'm sure they'll be talking to other people."

I shook my head. "There were people close enough at the other tables around us to have heard Ramsey talking about the

Newark cops and the FBI. Somebody will be curious, like we were, and dig up the truth. And then the whole group will know about it by the end of the day."

Will had started to frown as I talked. Now he sighed and said, "You're right. Something like this won't be kept quiet. Good Lord, what a terrible thing to happen to Ian."

"Yeah . . . assuming he didn't chop those guys up into little pieces."

"His brother confessed. The charges were dropped."

"And it's still possible he could be guilty. Terrence Keller could have known the details of the murders because Ian told him about them."

Will thought about it and nodded. "And he could have known where the bloody clothes were because Ian told him about that, too."

"It's more likely that they were Terrence's clothes, and they got bloody while he was helping his brother dispose of the bodies. That would make him an accessory after the fact, but not a killer. Why keep the clothes, anyway? Why not just burn them?"

"So he'd have some physical evidence that he could show the cops if he had to confess to save his little brother from prison?"

"Sounds reasonable to me," I said.

"But the police must have thought of these same things," Will objected.

"Sure they did. I imagine they had plenty of doubts. But with Terrence's confession and the bloody clothes, a jury would have enough reasonable doubt to acquit Ian if the case came to trial. They weren't gonna win that, and they knew it. So they dropped those charges and went with a case they could win."

He frowned at me. "You know too much about this stuff."

"I get most of it from movies and TV, like everybody else," I assured him.

"So what you're saying is that you think Ian murdered those men after all."

I shook my head. "I don't have any earthly idea. The story his brother told could be the gospel truth, for all I know. Criminals have done things a lot stupider than keeping blood-stained clothes."

"And even if he's guilty, I suppose that part of his life is so far in the past, it's almost like someone else committed those crimes."

"I don't know that I'd go so far as to say that."

"What I know is that I'll never be able to look at Ian quite the same again," Will said. "And neither will anyone else once this story gets around. Blast it, Delilah, this is going to ruin him, and it's not fair when we don't know for sure if he's guilty." His eyes widened as something else occurred to him. "But why did those detectives want to talk to him? No matter what happened in New Jersey twenty years ago, it can't possibly have anything to do with Howard Burleson and Tennessee Williams and *Cat on a Hot Tin Roof*!"

"You sure wouldn't think so," I said.

But deep down, I wasn't certain. Ian Keller might have committed at least two murders in the past. If that was true, I didn't think he would hesitate to get rid of an old man who got in the way of something he wanted.

But for the life of me, I couldn't figure out what that something might be.

CHAPTER 16

What with getting caught up in the story of Ian Keller's background, Will had almost forgotten that he was supposed to be on one of the festival panels that morning. He recalled it in time, though, and asked me if I was going to attend.

"What's it about again?" I asked.

"Williams's use of setting as character."

That didn't make much sense to me. You had your setting, and you had your characters, and they were two separate things, or at least so I'd always been taught in school. But I knew from experience that Will could make almost anything interesting, and I usually learned something from listening to him talk, too. So I said, "Sure, I'll come with you. I ought to let those detectives know where I'm going, though, in case they need to talk to me again."

It was possible Ramsey and Nesbit would forbid me to leave the hotel, in which case Will would just have to go on by himself. I didn't really expect that to happen. I had already told them everything I knew.

Well, almost everything. I still hadn't said anything to them about seeing Callie Madison in the garden right after I found Howard Burleson's body.

Will and I agreed to meet in the lobby in half an hour, then we would walk together to the museum where the festival's panels were being held. The museum, which housed a collection of items relating to New Orleans and its arts and history, had a small auditorium that was perfect for the panels, Will told me.

I went down early to see if I could find one or both of the detectives. Dale Gillette was behind the registration counter, talking to the clerks who were currently on duty. He must have spotted me as I headed in that direction, because he came out from behind the counter to meet me.

"Ms. Dickinson," he said. "How are you this morning? I hope you've recovered a little from the terrible experiences of last night."

"I'm all right," I told him. I looked around the lobby. "I thought the place was supposed to be thronged with reporters."

Gillette gave me a thin smile. "They got word that there's going to be a press conference at police headquarters to announce an arrest. I'm sure they'll be back later." He paused. "By the way, I took the liberty of having our operator screen the calls to your room. I have a list of messages for you, but they're all from reporters wanting an interview or at least a quote. You can return them or not, as you choose."

I was irritated for a second by Gillette's high-handed manner. He didn't have any right to screen my calls. But then I realized that to his way of thinking, he was just trying to do what he could to protect the privacy of one of the hotel's guests, so I supposed I couldn't be too upset with him. That explained, too, why my phone hadn't been ringing off the hook, which was something I'd wondered about.

"All right, thanks," I said. "I'll get that list from you later. Right now I'm looking for Detective Ramsey and Detective Nesbit. Are they still here?"

"Yes, they are. I'll show you the room they're using."

He led me to a small meeting room just off the lobby and knocked on the door. Ramsey, sounding annoyed, called from inside, "Yeah?"

Gillette opened the door a few inches and said, "Ms. Dickinson would like to speak to you, Detectives."

Nesbit came over and opened the door the rest of the way. He smiled at me and said, "Come in, Ms. Dickinson. Actually, we wanted to talk to you, so this is good timing." He nodded to Gillette and added, "Thanks."

"If there's anything you need, just let me know," Gillette said. He was eager to please because he was eager to get the cops out of the hotel.

Nesbit closed the door behind me. The room was simply furnished, with a long wooden table surrounded by eight straight-backed chairs, a few paintings on the walls, and a smaller table that held a pitcher of ice water and some glasses. Nesbit nodded toward them and asked, "Would you like something to drink?"

"No, thanks," I said. "I came to ask you if it would be all right for me to leave the hotel."

"No," Ramsey said flatly, but Nesbit asked, "Where did you want to go?"

"Just a few blocks away, to the museum where the festival's panels are being held."

Nesbit nodded. "I know the place. I think that would be all right, don't you, Detective Ramsey?"

Ramsey grunted and shrugged.

"Before you go, though," Nesbit went on, "what do you know about Dr. Ian Keller?"

I thought for a second about how to respond, then decided that lying wouldn't serve any purpose. "Before this morning, I didn't know anything about him except that he's from up north somewhere and is an English professor. But after that little scene in the ballroom, I looked him up on the Internet."

"So you know about his involvement with organized crime and the two murders in New Jersey?"

"Alleged involvement," I said. "The newspaper stories I read online sounded like nothing was ever proven against him."

Ramsey said, "He killed those two guys in Newark. Count on it. His brother just took the fall for him. But Terry Keller probably ordered those murders and who knows how many others, so I'm not gonna lose any sleep over him rotting in prison. I just wish his brother was in there with him."

"What's all that got to do with what happened to Howard Burleson?" I asked.

Nesbit crossed his arms over his chest and looked at me. "You tell us," he suggested.

"I can't tell you what I don't know," I replied with a shake of my head. "I don't see any way in the world Burleson could be connected with what happened in New Jersey twenty years ago. He was living in Atlanta then. He didn't seem to know Dr. Keller, and Keller didn't know him." I took a deep breath. "If you want my opinion, I think Keller just happened to be walking through the garden around the time of Burleson's murder. He's bound to not have been the only one."

"You think we questioned him only because of his ties to organized crime?" Nesbit asked.

"No, I think you questioned him because he was around the scene of the crime about the same time the murder took place." I waited a second, then added, "I think you came into the ballroom and embarrassed him because of what happened in the past."

"You got a mouth on you," Ramsey snapped.

"Must be the red hair," I told him as my eyes narrowed angrily.

Nesbit said, "All right, let's not start that again. Have you thought of anything else since last night that might help us?"

I shook my head. "No, I haven't. But what more help do you need? You've already arrested Tamara Paige, haven't you?"

"Dr. Paige is still in custody." It was Nesbit's turn to shrug. "She'll be arraigned shortly on a charge of first-degree murder. Luring Burleson down to the garden shows premeditation, and so does burning those manuscript pages to destroy evidence."

"So what was the deal with Dr. Keller?"

I didn't really expect either of them to answer me, but Ramsey grinned and said, "Fun."

That arrogance was too much for me. I blew up. "You've probably ruined the man's life for no good reason! How in the world can you call that fun?"

"He had it comin'," Ramsey insisted.

I just shook my head.

"We don't have to explain our actions to you, Ms. Dickinson," Nesbit said tightly. "But given Dr. Keller's record and his proximity to this crime, we would have been negligent in our duty if we didn't question him."

"Sure," I said. "Tell yourself whatever you need to hear."

"Go on to your panel," Nesbit said. "Just don't check out of the hotel or try to leave town."

"Don't worry, I'm not leaving New Orleans as long as the tour's still going on. I have a responsibility to my clients."

Ramsey said, "I guess that doesn't extend to keeping them from being murdered."

I got out of there before I took a swing at the obnoxious son of a gun. I had dealt with the cops more than I liked to think about in the past couple of years, but Ramsey was by far the biggest jackass among them.

Will was waiting in the lobby with a slightly worried look on his face. When he saw me, he smiled and said, "I thought you'd changed your mind, or that something came up."

"I checked with Ramsey and Nesbit to be sure it's all right for me to leave the hotel," I explained. "They said it was. Have you been waitin' long?"

Will shook his head. "No, just a few minutes. We still have plenty of time."

We left the hotel and started walking toward the museum. It was a beautiful morning in New Orleans. The air was cool, the sky a deep blue with white clouds floating in it. The French Quarter had a pleasantly drowsy feel to it, not surprising since a lot of the restaurants, clubs, and bars in the area were open until well after midnight. The Quarter's inhabitants were sleeping in this morning.

The museum was housed in a beautiful old building. I saw Jake Madison standing in front of it. He might have been admiring the architecture or just the techniques that the builders had used. He took a professional interest in such things, Callie had said earlier.

Jake glanced over at us as we walked up, then looked again and said, "Oh, hi, Ms. Dickinson. Dr. Burke."

"Hello, Mr. Madison," I said. "What do you think of the building?"

He grinned. "Callie told you I'm in construction, I'll bet. The guys who put this sucker up knew what they were doin'. They didn't have our modern techniques or equipment, but the place has been standing for well over a hundred years. Heck, some of these buildings are probably close to two hundred years old. You gotta admire the guys who built them."

"I talked to your wife this morning at the hotel," I told him. "She said you enjoyed your meal last night."

His smile widened into a grin. "Man, I ate so much I thought I was gonna pop!" He patted his stomach. "Luckily, I was able to sleep it off and have a big breakfast at the hotel this morning. The festival puts on a good feed. Only problem was that Callie was already gone by the time I got up, and I wanted to talk to her." He frowned and pointed at the museum. "She's on a panel here this morning, isn't she?"

Will nodded. "She's on the same one I'm on, as a matter of fact. She's probably inside by now. We'll see if we can find her."

"Okay, thanks." As the three of us started into the building, Jake added, "I was sure sorry to hear about that old guy gettin' killed last night. He seemed like a hoot."

"He was a nice man," I said.

"The cops know who did it yet?"

"I think they're supposed to announce something this morning," I told him, without mentioning what I knew about Tamara's impending arrest.

"Yeah, well, I hope they found the guy. Anybody who'd kill a nice old man deserves whatever they get."

I couldn't argue with that. But even as Jake said it, I wondered about Callie. I might have to come right out and tell her that I knew about her affair with Dr. Jeffords. If she wanted me to keep quiet and not say anything to the cops about her being in the garden the night before, she was going to have to convince me that she hadn't had anything to do with Burleson's murder.

Quite a few people were already in the museum, which had several galleries in addition to its auditorium. I saw Michael Frasier sitting forlornly in a corner, underneath a painting of a long-haired gentleman in a fancy outfit, possibly one of the founders of New Orleans. I thought about going over to him, but instead I just pointed him out to Will.

"Yeah, his presentation is scheduled right after the panel I'm on," Will said. "I don't know what he's going to do. Without anything to back up his theory, he'd probably be better off just cancelling the whole thing."

"What do you mean?" I asked.

"Well, everybody here knows he was going to claim that Mr. Burleson and Tennessee Williams were lovers. That's somewhat controversial, but it's well known that Williams had many short-lived romances. There's no way to prove or disprove that part of Burleson's story, and it's certainly not going to make or break Michael's career. He kept the part about Burleson claiming to have written *Cat on a Hot Tin Roof* under wraps, except for you, me, and Tamara knowing. When the story of her arrest gets out, so will the rest of it, and the circumstances certainly make it appear that Tamara believed Burleson was telling the truth. Most people in the academic world won't be convinced one way or the other, but after a while, the whole controversy will die down. Some scholars will probably support the theory, and others won't. But that's common, and Michael can carry on with his career. If he gets up there now, though, and springs the idea on everybody without any sort of proof, he won't have much support. That's why I said he'd be better off to wait."

I wasn't sure I understood all that, but Will was a lot more aware of the nuances of the academic world than I was, of course. I was willing to take his word for it.

"What if it turns out that Dr. Paige didn't kill the old man?" I asked.

Will frowned. "All the evidence points to her, doesn't it?"

"Maybe. Sometimes evidence can be interpreted different ways, though."

Will shook his head and said, "If Tamara is innocent, then it completely cuts the legs out from under Burleson's claims." He looked around. "Where'd Mr. Madison go?"

I hadn't noticed that Jake wasn't with us anymore. I'd gotten caught up in thinking about the murder again. I looked around the museum and didn't see him anywhere.

"Maybe he found his wife and is talking to her," I suggested.

Will nodded toward a pair of closed double doors. "Let's go on into the auditorium. The festival volunteers may still be setting up for the panel, but they won't run us out."

We went over to the doors, and Will opened one of them wide enough for us to slip through. As we did, I saw that the room had already been prepared for the panel. A folding table draped with a white cloth was on the stage with chairs behind it. A couple of hand microphones on stands sat on the table, along with some pitchers of water and glasses. Folded cardboard name placards sat in front of each chair. I saw Will's name on one of them and Callie's on another. The names of the other three panelists were familiar to me because I had seen them on the list of tour group members, but I hadn't really gotten to know any of them.

I took in all of that at a glance, but most of my attention was focused on Jake Madison, who was standing in front of a door that led to a backstage area. As I watched, he reached out, grasped the knob, twisted it, and flung the door open. I heard a woman gasp in surprise and thought, *Oh, no.*

"Somebody out front told me they'd seen you coming back here, Callie," Jake said in an angry, booming voice. "I figured I'd find the two of you together."

Beside me, Will asked, "What's going on here?"

"Nothin' good," I said.

Callie hurried out of the little hallway, followed by Dr. Andrew Jeffords. "Jake, what are you doing here?" she asked. "I . . . I thought you were going to look at old buildings, like you always do."

"No, I came to look at my cheating wife," Jake said. "Damn, Callie, I can't believe it! Jeffords? Really? This guy's old enough to be your dad!"

Jeffords stepped forward and said, "Mr. Madison, I swear this isn't what it looks like—"

"Yeah, guys always say that when they get caught kissing some other guy's wife, don't they?" Jake shook his head. "You know what, Doc? What I just saw was exactly what it looked like . . . and I know exactly what to do about it."

I knew from the menacing sound of Jake's voice that all hell was about to break loose. I took a quick step forward and said, "Mr. Madison, wait—"

Jake didn't wait, though. He swung a fist and sent it crashing right into Andrew Jeffords's face.

CHAPTER 17

Jeffords went flying backward and tripped over the steps leading up to the stage. Jake went after him, but Will leaped forward and grabbed him from behind, wrapping his arms around him. "Mr. Madison, stop it!" Will said. "Stop it!"

"Oh, my God!" Callie screamed. "Andrew!"

That expression of concern for Jeffords just made Jake even more furious. With an angry roar, he broke out of Will's grasp and went after Jeffords again. By now, though, Callie had gotten between them. "Leave him alone!" she said as she pushed at Jake's chest. "Leave him alone, damn it!"

Jake brought his left arm around. He didn't actually hit Callie, he just shoved her hard enough to make her stumble backward and then sit down hard on the floor. She let out a cry of pain as she landed.

Will caught hold of Jake's shoulder and hauled him around. Jake threw another punch, directed this time at Will for interfering. Will ducked under it and hooked a blow of his own into Jake's midsection. That was the first time I had ever seen Will hit anybody. I was surprised when Jake turned pale and doubled over. Will gave him a push that sent him sprawling on the floor in front of the stage.

Some of the people outside must have heard the commotion. The doors opened and curious faces peered in. Seeing three people down, several of the professors hurried in. I recognized the two who'd been arguing ever since we left Atlanta, but they weren't squabbling at the moment. They looked worried, instead.

"What's going on here?" one of them asked. "Is anyone hurt? Dr. Jeffords, what happened to you?"

Jeffords's glasses were askew and blood leaked from his nose. Callie scrambled up and hurried over to him. As she dropped to her knees beside him on the steps, she said, "Andrew, are you all right? I'm sorry, I'm so sorry, I had no idea that he knew . . ."

Gasping for breath, Jake sat up and said, "I know . . . all about it . . . you . . . you . . . I wasn't asleep last night, like you thought I was. I knew . . . when you snuck out . . . followed you . . . saw you go to that old bastard's room . . . I didn't want to believe it . . . but you didn't give me any choice."

If Jake had followed his wife the night before, that meant he could have been in the garden around the time of Howard Burleson's murder, too. That thought shot through my mind. And once Jake had confirmed his suspicions, he would have returned to their room ahead of Callie, so he could go back to pretending to be asleep.

I had no idea what had caused Callie to cheat on him. Obviously, he had a pretty violent temper, and from the first time I'd met them, the two of them hadn't seemed like a very good match to me. But I'd seen a lot of happy couples who don't have much in common, so I hadn't really thought about it until I'd spotted Callie on Dr. Jeffords's balcony last night.

Their personal life was none of my business. The fact that Jake had probably been in the garden around the time of the murder was. Well, not according to the cops, of course, but I considered it my business.

Right now, though, there was a commotion to smooth over. More people had crowded into the room, including some of the festival volunteers, and they wanted to know if anyone needed medical attention.

"I'm all right," Jeffords said. "Callie, help me up."

"Clearly you're not all right, Andrew. You're bleeding."

"I'll be fine," he insisted.

She helped him to his feet while Will extended a hand to Jake Madison. Jake hesitated, then took it and let Will help him up. Grudgingly, he said, "That was a heck of a punch for a professor."

"Just instinct and luck," Will said. "You tried to hit me and I struck back."

Jake turned to glare at Callie and Jeffords. "Now, you two—" he began.

"Not in here," I said. "Find someplace else to hash it out. There's a panel about to start in here."

"Thank you," one of the volunteers said to me. "Do we need to call the police to make sure there aren't any more disturbances?"

"Nah, I'm good," Jake said. "I gotta make some calls. I want to line up the best divorce lawyer in Atlanta before she gets her hooks into him."

"Jake!" Callie cried. "I . . . I don't want a divorce."

That made both Jake and Jeffords stare at her. After a moment, Jake said, "You got a funny way of showin' it, then."

"Outside," I said. "Talk about it outside."

Callie looked at me. "But . . . but I'm on this panel."

"We'll make do with four panelists," Will told her. "I don't think it's a good idea for you to try to continue."

"Dr. Burke is right, Callie," Jeffords said. "You have your own drama to play out, rather than discussing the ones written by Tennessee Williams."

Only a professor would say something like that, I thought . . . but Jeffords was right, no matter how he put it.

I managed to herd the three of them out of the auditorium. Will went as far as the doorway with us, where I paused and told him, "I was lookin' forward to hearin' what you had to say."

"I can give you the highlights later," he said with a smile. "Although I doubt if they'll be as exciting as the preliminaries."

"Huh," I said. "That kind of excitement I can do without."

It was sort of appropriate, though, I thought as I left the auditorium with Callie, Jake, and Jeffords, having so much drama at a Tennessee Williams Festival. We'd had lust, greed, fistfights, murder, and plenty of emotional turmoil. Maybe a little madness, too, depending on whether or not Howard Burleson's claims turned out to be true. If Williams had been writing all this, the language would have been fancier, but I was willing to bet he could have gotten enough material from this crazy bunch for a play or two.

I got the Madisons and Dr. Jeffords off in a corner and told them, "I'm not a marriage counselor or a referee, but I think you folks need to talk about this."

Jake grunted. "What is there to talk about? She cheated on me . . . and with a guy who looks like Orville Redenbacher, for Christ's sake!"

I was glad to see that I wasn't the only one who thought Dr. Jeffords bore an uncanny resemblance to the popcorn man. That didn't help the situation, though.

"Jake, I'm sorry," Callie said. "I know that doesn't mean anything to you right now, but I really am. I . . . I never meant for it to turn out this way. Andrew and I were working together and . . . and things just happened. You and I have grown so far apart—"

"Oh, hell," Jake broke in. "People always say that. It doesn't mean anything. You either honor your vows or you don't. Simple as that."

She looked down at the floor. "I know. You're right." Her eyes came back up and locked with his. "But I don't want a divorce. I know that, too."

Jake looked confused. "Well . . . what do you want?"

"To put all this behind us?"

"Callie?" Jeffords exclaimed. "Does this mean—"

She turned toward him. "I'm afraid it does, Andrew. We . . . we have to end it. I'm sorry." She swung back to Jake and reached out to put her hand on his arm. "Let's go back to the hotel and talk about it."

He looked steadily at her for a long moment, then heaved a sigh. "Yeah, I guess we ought to do that before we throw away fifteen years of marriage."

They started toward the door. I wanted to call out for them to wait. I hadn't asked them any questions about Burleson's murder. My mouth even opened.

But I didn't say anything. I supposed my investigation could wait. They were just going back to the hotel, not leaving town. Anyway, I couldn't really bring myself to believe that either of them had killed Howard Burleson. They just didn't have any reason to do that.

But they might have seen something that could lead to the killer, I reminded myself. That was the real reason I needed to talk to them.

"I . . . I don't believe it," Jeffords said as he stood beside me, watching Callie and Jake leave the museum. "She's abandoning me and going back to that . . . that savage."

My opinion of all of them wasn't very high at the moment, and that included Jeffords. Before I stalked off, I glared over at him for a second and said, "Oh, go pop some popcorn."

* * *

Since it hadn't taken long to get things settled down between Callie and Jake, I slipped back into the auditorium and caught most of the panel. As I expected, it was sort of interesting at times, at least when Will was talking. The other professors droned a little and I had to stifle a yawn or two.

When the panel was over, Will spent a few minutes talking to some of his colleagues who came up to him, then he noticed me waiting for him and excused himself. He came over to me and asked, "What happened with the Madisons and Dr. Jeffords?"

"Callie and Jake went back to the hotel to talk. She was still claiming that she didn't want a divorce, and I think there's at least a chance she can talk him into goin' along with that. I don't know where Dr. Jeffords went, and I don't care. What a dirty old man."

"Don't be too rough on him," Will said. "His wife died fairly young, while they were still in their forties. He's been a widower for almost twenty years. If some young, attractive woman started paying attention to him—"

"Don't make excuses for him," I said. "No matter how lonely he was, he knew she was married."

"Well, yeah, it's hard to get around that, isn't it?" Will admitted.

We were standing not far from the auditorium doors, which were open now between panels. One of the festival volunteers, an attractive, middle-aged, obviously well-to-do lady, came into the room, looked around, and spotted us. She came toward us with a worried look on her face, which prompted me to mutter, "Uh-oh."

"Dr. Burke," the woman said. "I need your help."

"Of course," Will said. "What can I do for you?"

"Talk to Dr. Frasier, please, and try to convince him to put on his presentation."

"He wants to cancel it?" Will asked. I remembered our earlier conversation.

"He says there's no point in it now," the volunteer said. "But that will leave us with a hole in the programming."

Will looked like he wished she hadn't tried to rope him into this. But I wasn't surprised when he nodded and said, "I'll see what I can do." It just wasn't in Will's nature to refuse when someone asked him for help. "No promises, though."

"Thank you, Dr. Burke."

We left the auditorium and saw Frasier standing in the museum lobby talking to three more volunteers—two men and another woman. As we walked over to join them, Frasier saw us coming and started to shake his head.

"Forget it, Burke," he said. "I'm not going through with it. There's no reason to get up there and humiliate myself."

I knew that Will sort of agreed with him, but for the good of the festival, he was willing to go against his instincts, or at least try to.

"Michael, no one blames you for what happened," he began. "You can at least get up there and talk about the time Mr. Burleson spent with Tennessee Williams in Italy. I know that as talkative as Mr. Burleson was, he must have related a number of stories about those days to you. And he said they spent some time here in the French Quarter as well. None of that is really controversial."

Stubbornly, Frasier shook his head. "It doesn't matter. You know what the centerpiece of my presentation was . . . the old man himself. Without him, no one is going to believe anything I say. Better to let it go so that everyone can just forget about it. All I want to do now is move on."

A part of me wanted to feel sorry for him, but I couldn't bring myself to do it. He had rubbed me the wrong way too many times.

Will said, "If you cancel your talk, Michael, people will remember you as a quitter."

"Better that than remembering me as a complete fool. Anyway, you know good and well that some other controversy will come along and make people forget about this one. That always happens."

Will shrugged. "Maybe."

"No maybe about it. After everything that's happened, it's better just to forget about it. And that's what I intend to do." Frasier looked at the festival volunteers. "Sorry."

One of the men sighed. "I suppose there's no way we can force you to go on stage and make your presentation, Dr. Frasier. But we're all very disappointed by your decision." He looked at the other volunteers. "I suppose we'd better make an announcement about the cancellation and post a sign for anyone who shows up later, so they'll know what's going on."

The volunteers went off to attend to those matters. Frasier gave Will and me a defiant glare and said, "I suppose you've lost all respect for me, haven't you?"

I figured that telling him I'd never respected him in the first place would just make things worse, so I kept my mouth shut. Will just said, "It was your decision, Michael. I respect that."

Frasier muttered, "This never would have happened if not for that bitch Tamara. I'll never forgive her."

I thought that with a first-degree murder charge hanging over her head, Tamara Paige had a lot more important things to worry about than whether or not Frasier forgave her. Again, though, it wasn't going to do any good to point that out.

Still muttering to himself, Frasier left the museum. With his presentation cancelled, nothing else was scheduled there until the afternoon. So as soon as one of the volunteers got on the public address system and made the announcement, the rest of the festival-goers started to filter out of the place, except for a handful who remained to look through the museum itself.

"We might as well go back to the hotel," I said to Will.

He nodded, looking a little glum. "Yeah. Between the murder and that scene Callie and her husband made, the festival's not getting off to a very good start."

I would have added the commotion during the opening ceremonies the night before to that list. And Howard Burleson had had a busy evening, first disappearing and then getting himself killed.

We left the museum and started back toward the St. Emilion. The streets were a little busier now as more tourists were out and about. This wasn't the height of tourist season in New Orleans, which was probably one reason the festival was scheduled for now.

"I probably ought to go see Dr. Paige," I said as we walked along past the picturesque buildings.

"Why?" Will asked.

"Well, I feel a certain responsibility toward her. She's a member of my tour group, after all, and when one of the folks you brought with you is in trouble, you want to help out. At least, I do."

"And you still don't believe she's guilty," Will said.

I shrugged. "I know all the evidence points to her. I want to make sure she has a good lawyer, though."

Will nodded and said, "I can understand that. I've known Tamara for several years and always liked her. I don't want her being railroaded if she's really innocent."

I heard the wail of a siren somewhere behind us. We stopped and turned to look. An ambulance came along the narrow street, moving fast but not at breakneck speed. It couldn't go too fast here in the French Quarter. The ambulance went past us with lights flashing and ambulance whooping, then turned a corner up ahead. A moment later, the siren stopped.

As the echoes faded, I realized that the ambulance had turned onto the same street where the hotel was located.

"Oh, shoot," I said.

Will looked over at me. "What? You don't think it has anything to do with our group, do you?"

"The way things have been goin', I wouldn't count on it," I replied grimly. Then I started hurrying along the sidewalk, almost breaking into a run. Will came after me and caught up easily.

We didn't say anything else until we rounded the corner. Then I saw the ambulance parked in front of the St. Emilion with its lights still flashing.

"We still don't know—" Will began. Then he stopped short. He knew as well as I did that this couldn't be anything good.

We found a crowd of people in the hotel lobby. The excitement of the ambulance's arrival had brought them out. I spotted Dale Gillette among them and went over to him.

"What happened?" I asked. "Is that ambulance here for one of my tour group?"

He nodded. "I'm afraid so, Ms. Dickinson. It's—"

Before he could finish, the elevator doors opened and the crew from the ambulance wheeled out a gurney with a big mounded shape on it that I recognized, even before Edgar and June Powers hurried out of the elevator behind the paramedics. One of the guys from the ambulance went ahead, clearing a path for the gurney. As it came closer, I saw the oxygen mask strapped over Dr. Lawrence Powers's face.

"Papa Larry," I breathed.

"Evidently he had a heart attack," Gillette said. "That's what I was told, anyway."

The gurney rolled past us, with Edgar and June following closely behind it. "This is all your fault," June was saying bitterly to her husband.

"How is it my fault?" Edgar asked.

"I don't know, but it is."

I fell in step beside Edgar and said, "If there's anything I can do to help, Dr. Powers—"

"You've done enough," June snapped. "Getting the police involved and stirring up everything with that murder probably put too much strain on Papa Larry's heart."

I thought that was completely unfair. I hadn't had any choice but to get the police involved once I found Howard Burleson's body. And I figured getting drunk as a skunk, not to mention having to put up with the bickering between his son and daughter-in-law, had put a strain on Larry's heart, too.

I didn't say anything, though. June was all worked up, so I just let it go. I stopped and watched the ambulance guys wheel the gurney on out of the hotel and load Papa Larry into the ambulance. Silently, I said a prayer for him.

Even if he survived this, he was still going to need all the help he could get.

But then, that was probably true of us all.

CHAPTER 18

There was nothing I could do for Larry Powers, so I figured the best thing would be for me to concentrate on something I might be able to affect. I called a cab to take me to the New Orleans police headquarters so I could see Tamara.

Will insisted on coming along and, to tell the truth, I didn't argue with him much. I knew I'd feel more comfortable if he was with me.

The cab driver knew where the police department was located, not surprisingly, and took us to the office on South Broad Street. Inside, an officer at the reception desk called Homicide to see if Detectives Ramsey and Nesbit were there. As it turned out, they weren't. The officer offered to take a message for them, but instead I asked where a female prisoner who had been arraigned this morning on a murder charge would be held pending a bail hearing.

"Y'all lookin' for that lady professor who killed the old man in the Quarter?" the cop asked.

"You've heard about the case?" I said.

The cop grinned. "Sure. Word gets around about somethin' like that. Most of our homicides are bar fights, one drug dealer shootin' another drug dealer, robberies gone wrong, things like that. I don't recall ever hearin' about a homicide involvin'

Tennessee Williams before. Y'all friends o' that lady professor?"

"That's right," Will said.

"She's been transferred to the custody of the Criminal Sheriff's Office. They'll have her over at the South White Street facility. You know where that is?"

We didn't, of course. The officer gave us directions, and we found another cab.

The place was as dreary and depressing as any jail anywhere, a sprawling building with bars on many of the windows and a fence topped by barbed wire on the roof. We went through plenty of red tape and metal detectors inside before I was allowed to see Tamara.

Will had to wait outside in an ugly little anteroom while I went into an even smaller room that was even uglier. It was divided in two by a counter with a single chair on each side. A wire-mesh-reinforced glass wall rose from the middle of the counter, and there was a phone on each side of the glass. After a few minutes, the door on the other side opened and a deputy brought Tamara in. She wore a short-sleeved white jumpsuit and had the sort of downcast expression you'd expect to see on the face of a prisoner, especially one facing serious charges. They didn't come much more serious than murder, I supposed.

She managed a smile when she saw me, though. We picked up our phones at the same time, and I said, "Hi."

"It's good to see a friendly face in here, Ms. Dickinson, or at least a nonhostile one. Thank you for coming."

"Call me Delilah," I said. "They treatin' you all right?"

Tamara shrugged. "As well as can be expected, I suppose."

"Do you have a lawyer yet?"

"I had a court-appointed one to handle the arraignment.

She's supposed to do the bail hearing, too. After that, I'll try to find a defense attorney of my own." She gave a short, bitter laugh. "Assuming, of course, that I can make bail and get out of here. Since I'm from out of town, the judge may consider me a flight risk and deny bail."

"We'll try to see that that doesn't happen," I promised. I lowered my voice a little and went on, "Do you know why they arrested you?"

"Something about some evidence they found in my hotel room. Ashes in the sink in the bathroom? That's crazy. I didn't burn anything in there."

"Ramsey and Nesbit found a little scrap of partially burned paper that looked like it came from a legal pad. Frasier said those pages from Howard Burleson's manuscript came from a legal pad."

Tamara closed her eyes for a moment and rubbed her temples with her free hand. "I never saw any manuscript pages, and I certainly never burned them. I wouldn't have had any reason to. If they even existed, they were fakes."

"You still believe that?"

"I don't have any reason not to believe it."

"The police think you saw them, realized that Burleson was telling the truth, and killed him and destroyed the pages to keep anyone from bein' able to prove that the old man wrote *Cat on a Hot Tin Roof*."

She shook her head. "I didn't do it, Delilah. I don't know what else to say. I didn't do it."

"It'd sure be helpful if you had an alibi."

"But I don't. I told you, I went back to my room, couldn't sleep, and decided to work out for a while. I was alone the whole time."

"Well," I said, thinking back to the night before, "you

stepped out to get some ice from the machine, because that's what you were doing when I ran into you. Did you leave your room any other time?"

"No, that was the first time I'd been out of the room for several hours and, as you said, I just stepped out. The room was just down the hall from the ice machine, so I threw the deadbolt to keep the door from closing and walked down there with the ice bucket."

I knew what she meant. I had done the same thing in hotels many times myself.

"It doesn't sound like you've got an alibi," I admitted with a sigh.

Tamara shook her head. "Not even a ghost of one. But I give you my word, Delilah, I didn't kill that old man." She smiled faintly. "It would be nice if at least one person believed that."

"I do," I said without hesitation.

"Now all you have to do is convince everyone else."

Unfortunately, I couldn't see any way to do that. There wasn't much in the way of physical evidence, just that bit of ash from the sink in Tamara's bathroom, but it pointed straight at her.

"I'll do my best," I told her anyway. "I'll see about getting you a better lawyer for the bail hearing, too."

"I should warn you, I'm not a rich woman."

"I'm not, either, but I want to do whatever I can to help."

I said a few more encouraging words, then told her goodbye and left the depressing little room. If it was that depressing for me, I thought, how much worse must a cell be for Tamara? I could get up and walk out, but she couldn't.

"Was she able to tell you anything that might help?" Will asked as we made our way back out of the jail.

"Not really. She says she didn't kill the old man and that

she never saw any manuscript pages from that play. She still doesn't believe that Burleson really wrote it, either."

"What about bail?"

"We'll have to wait and see. I promised that I'd try to get her a defense lawyer, and not just a court-appointed one."

Will nodded. "If you need help with the money, I've got some savings."

"You'd dip into your savings to help Tamara?"

"We're friends," he said, and I felt an unexpected pang of jealousy. I knew that Tamara had once been involved with Michael Frasier. I wondered if there had ever been anything going on between her and Will. She was a pretty attractive woman, after all. But I didn't want to come right out and ask him.

Anyway, I'd offered to help pay for a good lawyer, too, just because I thought she was innocent. Maybe Will felt the same way. I sure as heck didn't want to generate any more drama on this trip. There had been way more than enough already.

We took another cab back to the hotel. When we got there, we went to Dale Gillette's office and Will knocked on the door. Gillette told us to come in.

"Have you had any word about Dr. Powers?" I asked him.

"Yes, I called the hospital and checked on him a short time ago," Gillette said. "They wouldn't tell me anything, of course, since I'm not a relative, but I persuaded them to page Dr. Edgar Powers, so I was able to talk to him. He told me that his father is in serious but stable condition."

I was glad to hear that Larry hadn't died from the heart attack, at least not yet. He wasn't one of my favorite people in the world, nor were June and Edgar, but I didn't want any more members of my group dying. And despite Larry's bullheadedness and fondess for the booze, I sort of liked him. He was a colorful character, and we Southerners have always had a fondness for colorful characters. The plays of Tennessee Williams are proof of that.

Gillette went on, "We're still getting quite a few calls from reporters for you, Ms. Dickinson. You might want to consider issuing a statement to the press."

That didn't sound like a good idea to me. I didn't want to reinforce the idea even more of my name being linked to murder. That couldn't be good for business.

I thanked Gillette for his suggestion anyway, without promising to do anything about it, and Will and I left the office. By now it was past noon—almost one o'clock, in fact—and it had been quite awhile since the unfinished breakfast buffet that morning. I said, "Why don't we get some lunch?" and Will was in total agreement.

Neither of us was in the mood for something from the hotel's restaurant, so we left the St. Emilion and started wandering the streets of the French Quarter. We found a little Cajun place a couple of blocks away, not much more than a hole in the wall, but it was doing a brisk business, even past the lunch rush. We stood in line for a few minutes to get a table, and when the food came, we found out why the café was busy. The crawfish gumbo, the rice and red beans, the blackened fish, all of it was delicious, and spicy enough to bring tears to your eyes. I must have drunk nearly a gallon of sweet tea during the meal to try to put out the fire.

We didn't make a deal not to talk about the murder while we were eating or anything like that, but the subject didn't really come up. Maybe we were both just tired of trying to figure out if Tamara Paige was really guilty, and, if she wasn't, who had killed Howard Burleson. We talked about other things instead: books, movies, our families, the same sorts of things anybody would talk about during a pleasant lunch with someone they cared a lot about.

It was such a nice interlude that when we were finished, I didn't really want to go back to the hotel. "Can't we just sit here and sip sweet tea for the rest of the afternoon?" I asked Will with a smile.

"I wish we could," he said, "but there are readings tonight, and I'm supposed to take part. I'm going to be reading one of Williams's short stories, and I ought to look it over before-hand."

"All right," I said with a smile and a sigh. "Can't keep an English professor away from the books for very long, can you?"

Will laughed. "You think that afterwards we could go back to that same place where we ate last night?"

"I'll call them when we get back to the hotel and see if I can get a reservation for us," I promised.

And this night was going to end differently, I told myself. No drunken theater professors, no cheating wives, no alleged mobsters from New Jersey, and, most of all, no dead bodies or cops. Instead, I was thinking that I might just ask Will to have breakfast with me in the morning . . . room service breakfast.

As we walked through the hotel lobby a short time later, someone called Will's name as we passed a group of festival-goers sitting on one of the sofas. "Dr. Burke, can we get your opinion on something?"

I saw the two argumentative professors in the middle of the bunch, and when Will smiled at me and said, "This is liable to take awhile," I knew exactly what he meant.

"I'm gonna go on up to the room," I told him. "I'll see you later."

As I went toward the elevators, I glanced along the broad corridor that led to the atrium and the indoor garden. I was tempted to go out there and look again at the place where I'd found Burleson's body, but I knew it might still be cordoned off as a crime scene. Besides, the forensics team from the police department would have been all over it and taken any possible evidence with them. I stopped at the elevators instead and pushed the button.

Where the murder had taken place wasn't that important, I told myself as I waited. The garden was just a convenient spot where the killer had managed to get some privacy. Would Burleson have gone out there with just about anybody he knew? I suspected he would have. The old man had been friendly and garrulous, and he hadn't seemed to have a suspicious bone in his body. He was the sort of old-fashioned Southern gentleman who would talk to anybody, anywhere, about anything. Luring him to the scene of his death wouldn't have been a problem.

But there was something else nagging at me, and I couldn't figure out what it was. Something I had seen or heard—or both—that didn't quite jibe with the facts. I frowned with the effort as I tried to force my brain to grasp it.

Then the elevator arrived, and all I could do was shake my head and get on board. Whatever that elusive discrepancy was, it had gotten away from me.

As I walked along the third floor hall, one of the doors ahead of me swung open and Dr. June Powers stepped out into the corridor. She looked drawn and haggard, and I wasn't surprised. She didn't see me at first, but then she noticed me and stopped short.

"Ms. Dickinson," she said as the door clicked shut behind her. She heard it and looked around. "Damn it," she said. "I hope I haven't locked myself out. I was just going down to the vending machines to get a candy bar. I didn't have a chance to eat any lunch today."

"I'm sorry," I said. "How's your father-in-law?"

"Still stable. Still in serious condition." She didn't have her purse with her, but she reached into the pocket of her slacks and pulled out a key card. "Good. I won't have to call the desk to let me in. I couldn't remember if I had the key or not."

"If there's anything I can do—"

"Yes, you make that offer frequently, don't you?"

The words were sharp and got under my skin. I was about to say something when she shook her head and went on. "I'm sorry, that was uncalled for. Of course you try to be helpful. That's your job."

"That's right," I said.

"And I should apologize for what I said to you earlier, too. I know logically that you didn't have anything to do with Papa Larry's heart attack. In fact, I'm not really surprised it happened, considering how long he's been abusing his body the way he does. He smoked for years, in addition to the drinking, and the man is grossly overweight. Cancer, heart attack, stroke . . . something's bound to do him in before too much longer if he doesn't change his ways. It may be too late already."

She had the sort of sanctimonious disapproval in her voice that always gets on my nerves. I'd never had any trouble with smoking or drinking, since I'd never smoked and was only a light social drinker, and as long as I watched what I ate, my weight wasn't a problem, but I understood that some people didn't have it as lucky. It was easy to tell somebody else what they ought to do, I thought. It was a lot harder to figure out what *you* ought to do to improve your own life, and then stick to it.

But I didn't want to get in an argument with June. She had been through enough today already. Instead, I said, "Did your husband stay at the hospital?"

She nodded wearily. "Edgar thought I ought to come back here and rest for a while. Then I'll go back and let him have a break. I'm afraid our participation in the festival has come to a premature end."

"I'm sure nobody will hold that against you," I told her.

She looked at the key card she held in her hand. "Well, I'm going to go get that candy bar, and then maybe try to take a nap. We're going to be putting in some long hours sitting with Papa Larry."

I nodded, smiled, and moved on toward my room while June went the other way toward the alcove where the vending machines and the ice machine were. Thinking about it made me remember that Tamara had been on her way there with the ice bucket from her room the previous night, just before Ramsey and Nesbit came along and arrested her.

When I got to my room, I realized that I was tired, too. I stretched out on the bed for a while and dozed off. I might have had dreams, but if I did, I don't remember any of them.

I woke up and checked the time, since I wasn't sure how long I had slept. It was almost five o'clock, I saw to my surprise. But I'd been up very late the night before, I told myself, and hadn't slept all that well when I'd finally got to bed. It wasn't any wonder that I was tired.

I stood up, stretched, and walked over to the French doors. I pushed the curtains back, unlatched the doors, and stepped out onto the little balcony. The skylights above the garden were dim and gray, telling me that the sky was overcast, which of course wasn't uncommon here in New Orleans, as close to the Gulf as it was. The humidity was nearly always high, and that meant clouds.

Resting my hands on the ornate railing around the balcony, I looked down at the thick vegetation below me. I didn't see anyone moving around on the paths. I was sure that word had gotten around the hotel about Howard Burleson's body being found there, and I figured that people didn't regard the place as being nearly as romantic as they might have before. It would take awhile, a week or so, maybe, before the natural turnover of guests meant that most of the folks staying here wouldn't think of the garden as a murder scene. Then it would be busy again with people drinking, talking, and romancing.

Actually, I did hear someone talking, but only faintly. I thought at first that the voice originated down in the garden, but then I realized that it was coming from somewhere else. I wasn't sure where that could be, but then I looked along the row of balconies and saw a pair of French doors standing partially open. Somebody in that room was talking, I realized, and the high-ceilinged atrium caught the words, amplifying them and causing them to echo slightly. But the echo also distorted them a little.

But that didn't stop me from catching the word "Tennessee."

My hands tightened on the railing. There was something familiar about that voice, all right, and when I made out "tin roof," I suddenly knew what it was, even though it was so impossible it might have made me physically stagger if I hadn't been clutching the railing so hard.

The man talking was Howard Burleson.

CHAPTER 19

I stood there listening, hanging on to the railing for sanity. There was no way Howard Burleson could be alive. I had seen the blood on his head, gazed into his eyes that held no life. The body had been taken away, and it wasn't coming back.

Yet there was no doubt in my mind about what I was hearing. And as I realized the only way I could be hearing him talking right now, everything else shifted around in my brain and then locked down into place. I knew who had killed the old man, and I had a pretty good idea why.

And I knew that if I didn't act fast, the only proof might be gone forever.

I turned and ran back into my room, ran to the door and jerked it open. A moment later I was down the hall, knocking on the door of Michael Frasier's room.

He was slow to answer. I knocked again, harder and more insistently this time and, after a moment, he jerked the door open. "What is it?" he demanded in a surly voice.

"I just wanted to see how you were doin' after what happened today," I said. "I'm sure sorry that things didn't work out for you at the festival."

He started to close the door. "I'm fine. Now, if that's all . . ."

I put a hand on the door to stop it. "You know, you were right," I said.

"Right? About what?"

"Since you didn't do your presentation, this whole ugly business about Mr. Burleson will blow over after a while. I don't know much about academia, but I do know human nature. You learn a lot about it when you're in the travel business. And folks will always move on to something else, as long as there's nothin' to remind them of what happened."

I was babbling a little, but he just nodded and said, "Yeah, yeah, you're right. I appreciate the concern. Now, if you don't mind, I'm busy—"

"Doin' what? If I remember the festival schedule correctly, you don't have anything else lined up."

I didn't care about his plans for the rest of the festival. What concerned me was what he was about to do right now. I could make a pretty good guess about that and, as I talked, I tried to look past him into the room, searching for confirmation that my hunch was right.

I found it in the little palm-size digital recorder that I spotted lying on the table next to his computer.

"Actually, I thought maybe I could talk my way into the symposium that's being held tomorrow," Frasier said. He frowned in thought for a second, then pulled the door wide open. "Would you mind coming in for a minute, Ms. Dickinson? I'd like to talk to you about Dr. Burke."

That request surprised me. I didn't know what Will had to do with this. I wanted to find out, though, and, more importantly, I wanted to get my hands on that recorder. I said, "Sure," and stepped into the room. "What about Will?"

Frasier closed the door and started pacing. "I know he has a lot of influence with the festival committee and the other professors. He could get me into that symposium. And if I'm not mistaken, you have a lot of influence with him. You could per-suade him to speak up for me."

"I'm sure you could talk to him yourself, and he'd be glad to help." I edged toward the table while Frasier walked over to the French doors, which stood open onto the balcony. I kept talking to cover any sounds I made as I slipped my hand over the little recorder and then slid it off the table. "Why don't I go find him and tell him you want to talk to him?" I started toward the door. "You just wait right here—"

He turned and lunged across the room after me. I realized then that it had been a trick, that he'd gotten suspicious of my visit and had been waiting to see if I went for the recorder. I let out a little yelp and raced for the door, but he was too fast for me. His hand closed around my arm and jerked me back. He flung me across the room so that I landed on the king-size bed and bounced a little on the thick mattress.

"You bitch!" he said in a low, furious voice as he loomed over me. "What do you think you're doing? Stealing my recorder?"

"I . . . I'm sorry," I said, desperately trying to think of some explanation. "I'm a kleptomaniac! I can't help myself! I see something like that and I just pick it up!"

He didn't believe me, of course. Heck, I wouldn't have be-lieved me, especially if I were trying to hide the evidence that I was a murderer.

Which was exactly what Dr. Michael Frasier was. He had killed Howard Burleson.

He reached down and shoved his hand in the pocket of my trousers, going after the recorder. I swung a fist at his head, but he ducked, shoved me down against the mattress again, and yanked the recorder out of my pocket, ripping the fabric in the process.

"All right," he said through gritted teeth. "You want to hear what's on here so bad, I'll let you listen to some of it."

He pushed the PLAY button on the recorder, and I heard Howard Burleson's reedy voice again, saying, ". . . showed Tom the manuscript. I never dreamed he would really like it, but he did. He said it showed real promise."

Frasier clicked the recorder off and said, "Real promise. That's what my career held once. And it was going to again, once I became famous for discovering the hidden author of one of the most famous plays of the twentieth century. I guess that's why I was listening again, one more time, before I erased what's on the chip. I wanted to pretend that the dream hadn't been ruined forever."

"You did record Mr. Burleson's story," I said. "You lied about that. You lied about a lot of things."

He looked like he wanted to hit me. I was judging the angles to see if I could kick him in the groin when he controlled himself and backed off a little.

"I was lied to first," he said in a voice that trembled with anger. "That damned old man made a fool out of me. He made me believe his story, when it was all a pack of lies."

"He didn't know Tennessee Williams?" I figured it might be better to keep Frasier talking, to let him get as much of it off his chest as he would. Somebody else might come along and knock on the door and, if they did, I planned to scream my head off.

"He probably did," Frasier said. "He claimed to have photos of the two of them together, but he was coy about that, wouldn't show them to me. Williams could have picked him up in Italy, or vice versa. No doubt about that. It was the whole *Cat on a Hot Tin Roof* business that was a lie."

"How do you know? You saw the pages—"

He made a slashing motion with his hand. "Fakes! He just

copied a few pages from a published version of the play to have something to fool me with. He was supposed to bring the whole thing with him, but he didn't do it."

"You said he just brought samples," I said.

A cold smile curved his mouth. "That was going to be part of the surprise. I planned to display the entire manuscript at my presentation, but when I asked him for it last night, he admitted that he didn't have it. He said that something had happened to it, that it had disappeared somehow, back in Atlanta, and he'd been afraid to tell me. That was when I started to suspect that he was trying to pull some sort of scam. He had already weaseled quite a bit of money out of me, along with all the attention. He was going to let me get up there and make a fool of myself in front of all my colleagues."

That didn't sound like Burleson to me. I had heard him talking about writing that play, and whether it was true or not, I would have bet money that he believed it was.

"Maybe he really did lose the rest of the manuscript," I suggested. "That was no reason to . . . to . . . ."

"To kill him?" Frasier smiled down at me again. "No, I suppose not. But I lost my temper when we were talking about it in the garden. He had already wandered off again, after he told me he didn't have the manuscript and we'd argued about it, and that's where I found him. I didn't really mean to hurt him. I just got so mad I hauled off and hit him, and when he went down all I could see was my career in ruins, so I hit him a couple more times. You see, I'm not really a killer."

"But since he was already dead, you got the idea of framing Dr. Paige for it," I guessed.

"As far as anyone knew, she had a lot more to gain from his death than I did," Frasier said.

"So you spied on her and waited for your chance, and after the cops arrested her, you went to her room and burned a few little scraps from one of the manuscript pages, just enough to leave some evidence the police could find. You were able to get in because she'd left the deadbolt out to keep the door from closing all the way while she went to the ice machine. When you left, though, you let it shut and lock behind you."

That was the thing I'd been struggling to grasp earlier. I'd seen Detective Nesbit use a key card he'd gotten from Dale Gillette to open Tamara's door and hadn't really thought anything about it at the time. But when Tamara mentioned leaving the deadbolt out, that had jogged something in my memory. The discrepancy meant that somebody had been inside Tamara's room between the time of her arrest and the time when Ramsey had found the ashes in her sink.

Anyway, I realized now, nobody could have burned several whole pages from a legal pad in that bathroom without the smoke setting off the fire alarm. With the ventilator fan running, though, it might have been possible to burn a few tiny scraps and leave the ashes in the sink as evidence. All of that had come together in my mind as I stood on the balcony of my room earlier listening to Howard Burleson's voice on the recorder. I knew at that moment that Frasier had lied about not recording Burleson's story, and if he had lied about that, he could have lied about everything else, too.

Frasier shook his head as he glared down at me. "I didn't expect anyone to figure out what happened, and certainly not you."

I didn't waste time feeling insulted. I had bigger problems.

So did Frasier. He went on, "Now what am I going to do with you?"

"Nothing," I said. "Will knows I'm here. He'll be comin' along any minute lookin' for me."

"I don't think so. I have a better feel now for when someone's lying to me . . . and you're lying, Ms. Dickinson. I don't know how you found out about it, but you wanted to get your hands on that recorder. You think that's going to prove some-how that I'm a killer."

"You just admitted it to me."

He chuckled. "That's not proof."

"But I bet it'll be enough to get Tamara Paige off the hook for that murder charge," I went on. "And I reckon Ramsey and Nesbit will start lookin' a lot harder at you. No matter how careful you were, they'll find a fingerprint or something else to prove you were in Tamara's room. They'll figure out that you planted that evidence—and why."

His jaw tightened. "You've just talked yourself into taking a dive off that balcony out there."

I went cold all over.

"Yeah, you were upset because of the murder happening on a tour you set up," he said. "You figured it was going to ruin your business. So you committed suicide. Jumped right off your balcony into that garden. Our rooms are close enough, nobody will be able to tell that you came from here instead of there."

"That . . . that's only a three-story drop," I said. "You can't be sure a fall like that will kill somebody, especially with those plants down there."

He nodded. "You're right. That's why I think I'd better break your neck before I toss you through the doors and over the railing."

My eyes darted toward the French doors. The balcony was narrow enough so that he could do that, all right. He could get a running start and give me a good hard shove from inside the room, so that no one would see what he was doing. Someone on another balcony might see me fall, but I knew how unreli-able eyewitness testimony could be. Chances were, they wouldn't be able to swear which balcony I'd fallen from.

Frasier held up the recorder. "Then I'll erase what's on here, and no one else will ever have any reason to suspect me. Like you said, it'll all blow over, and I can carry on with my career. Sure, there'll be a stain on it, at least for a while, but I'll come up with something else to rebuild my reputation."

"Will Burke knows me well enough to know that I'd never kill myself," I said.

"But he won't be able to prove that, will he? And since the police don't suspect me of anything, there won't be any investigation targeted at me."

Who knew an English professor could be so blasted diabolical?

He leaned over the bed. "Don't make this any more difficult than it has to be."

The heck with that. I was gonna make killing me as difficult as I possibly could.

So I kicked him in the balls.

He let out a strangled howl of pain and doubled over. I lunged off the bed and grabbed at the recorder, wrenching it out of his hand. Before I could make a run for the door, though, he flung out an arm and caught hold of the collar of my blouse, then slung me backward. I hit the floor and slid along it, although I didn't go very far because the carpet was so thick it slowed me down.

Frasier was between me and the door now, so I knew I couldn't get out that way. Instead, as I scrambled to my feet and he stumbled toward me, I headed for the balcony instead. I planned to get out there and start screaming so loud that they'd hear me all the way out in the lobby. Frasier wouldn't dare kill me then.

He caught up to me just as I reached the doors and looped an arm around my neck from behind, silencing any scream I might have let loose. I rammed my elbows back at him, trying to break free as we staggered out onto the balcony. I still had the recorder clutched in my fingers, so I let fly with it, flinging it out into the atrium so that it would fall into the garden. Frasier cursed bitterly in my ear when he saw me do that.

Then I clamped onto the railing with both hands and held on for dear life as he tried to drag me back into the room. I had to keep us out here where somebody might see us. If he got me in the room again, he would break my neck, just as he had threatened a few moments earlier.

It was a deadly struggle, but one fought in silence except for a few grunts and the sound of our shoes scraping on the floor of the balcony. I kept waiting and hoping to hear somebody yell, "Look! That man's trying to kill that woman!"

But it didn't happen. It was dinnertime. Most folks were out eating somewhere. Frasier's arm tightened on my neck. He was going to choke me to death, right here in the middle of a crowded hotel.

But that would leave too many marks, and the coroner would be able to tell that I'd died of asphyxiation, not a broken neck—and Frasier still hadn't given up on his plan to make my death look like suicide. He hammered his other fist against the side of my head. The blow stunned me enough to make me go limp. Frasier started dragging me back toward the room. He could get away with punching me in the head. Any marks that left could be put down to an injury suffered in the fall. I was still trying to fight, but I wasn't doing much good now.

We had just gotten back to the French doors when I heard Dale Gillette exclaim, "Oh, my God!"

Frasier let go of me and twisted around. I slumped to the floor, half in the room, half on the balcony. My vision was a little blurry from being choked, but I saw Gillette standing in the hall with the key card he had just used to unlock the door still in his hand. Behind him stood Dr. Ian Keller, who bellowed, "I told you I saw him trying to kill Ms. Dickinson!" Keller started to push past Gillette with his fists clenched.

Frasier panicked and turned to flee from Keller, who charged into the room like a maddened bull. I don't know where he thought he was going to go. The balcony didn't offer anyplace to hide. But I grabbed his legs anyway, just to eliminate any chance of him getting away.

That was all I intended to do. I didn't mean for him to fall forward, crash into the railing, and flip right over it. I swear I didn't. But once he started to fall, there was no way I could hold him. With a terrified yell, he disappeared.

That yell lasted just a second before it ended in a loud thump. I winced, knowing what that meant.

I hoped the crazy son of a gun hadn't landed on anybody. He had already hurt enough people here in New Orleans.

CHAPTER 20

As it turned out, Frasier hadn't landed on anybody. He had come down at the edge of the marble walk around the outside of the garden. Another couple of feet and some shrubs would have broken his fall.

As it was, he broke his back and his left leg and gave himself one heck of a concussion. The doctors figured he would be paralyzed from the waist down, probably for the rest of his life.

That wouldn't keep him from going to prison, though.

Ramsey and Nesbit were mad at me, of course, especially Ramsey, but they found the recorder where I'd tossed it down into the garden. As Frasier had pointed out, the fact that Howard Burleson's voice was on there, talking about how he'd written *Cat on a Hot Tin Roof*, didn't really prove anything, but the way he'd tried to kill me did, especially since the forensics team was able to match the DNA of a hair they had found in Tamara's bathroom with Frasier's DNA. Faced with that, he confessed to killing Burleson in a fit of rage after the old man told him that the manuscript, except for a few sample pages he'd been keeping in a separate place, was gone.

According to what Frasier told the cops, Burleson had been

keeping the rest of the manuscript in a hollowed-out old family Bible he used as a hidey-hole. When Burleson went to get it before leaving for New Orleans, he found that it was gone, but he'd been afraid to tell Frasier. At least, that was what Burleson had claimed later, when he had broken down and let it slip to Frasier. Frasier had lost his head, assumed that everything the old man had told him before was a lie, and wound up killing him. That had been a crime of rage.

Framing Tamara Paige for the murder was more cold and calculated, an idea that had come to Frasier once he realized that he had beaten Burleson to death.

Frasier had come close to getting away with both of those crimes, as well as killing me, but Ian Keller had spotted us struggling on the balcony and gone for help. Luckily, he had run into Dale Gillette on the same floor and had been able to convince Gillette to open Frasier's door. It was a good thing for me that Dr. Keller looked so much like a mobster. He could be pretty intimidating when he wanted to.

The rest of the festival went off without any problems. The last I heard, Callie and Jake Madison had reconciled and put Callie's infidelity behind them. It probably helped that Callie resigned her position at the university and found a job at a college in Florida, and Jake moved his construction company down there, too. Dr. Larry Powers recovered from his heart attack, gave up drinking, and lost weight. Will kept me informed and told me that he was doing fine. That wasn't the case with his son and daughter-in-law. Junebug and Edgar split up. Probably the best thing for both of them, if you ask me.

I never found out if Ian Keller killed those two fellas in New Jersey. The law said he hadn't, and his brother is still in prison, serving that twenty-five-to-life sentence for the crimes, so there you go. All I know is that he'd saved my life, and I am grateful to him for that.

And there was one more thing that happened, the day after we all got back to Atlanta from New Orleans . . .

The sun was bright and warm enough for a spring day that I was glad to be standing in the shade of a tree next to the gravesite where the burial service for Howard Burleson had just been concluded. The lush green hills of the cemetery rolled away around us as Will and Tamara Paige and I waited to speak to Natalie Drummond. Natalie was a brunette in her thirties. She stood with her husband's arm around her as she shook hands with the mourners.

There weren't very many of them. Not a lot of Burleson's family had shown up for the funeral, and I thought that was a shame. Not very surprising, though, considering what he had told us about how they'd never accepted him.

When the others had left, Will and Tamara and I went over to introduce ourselves and pay our respects. Natalie managed a smile as she shook hands with us.

"I was hoping you'd come," she said. "I've heard about what you did for my grandfather, Ms. Dickinson."

"I'm not sure I did anything," I replied with a shake of my head.

"You found out who killed him and made sure that the man will pay." Natalie sighed. "And it's all so senseless."

"Murder usually is."

"Yes, of course, but I meant in this case, it was because . . . because of that manuscript . . ."

She started to cry. Her husband tightened his arm around her and said, "Honey, please don't do this to yourself. I've told you and told you, it's not your fault. You were just trying to help him."

Will frowned and said, "Wait a minute. What are you talking about, Mrs. Drummond?"

"The manuscript," Natalie said. "The one that Grandpa Howard hid in that old Bible."

"There really was a manuscript of *Cat on a Hot Tin Roof?*" Tamara asked.

Natalie nodded. "I didn't know what it was at the time, though. I just saw that it was a bunch of papers."

Will's voice held a hush that had nothing to do with our surroundings as he asked, "What did you do with them?"

"Well, I thought they might be important, and it didn't seem like an old Bible was anyplace to keep them, so I took them and put them in our safety deposit box. I was going to tell Grandpa Howard, but then . . . but then I got busy and it slipped my mind, and I never did think to tell him before he left to go to New Orleans with that awful Dr. Frasier."

I could see why she blamed herself for her grandfather's death. She'd had a hand in it, all right, but only indirectly, and certainly not intentionally. Anyway, the ultimate responsibility lay with the man who had struck Howard Burleson down, and he was still in the hospital in New Orleans, destined never to walk—or breathe free air—again.

"You put the manuscript in your safety deposit box?" Will said.

Tearfully, Natalie nodded again. "That's right. But I have it . . ." She put her hand into the big purse she carried and brought out a manila envelope. "Here. There are some pictures in it, too, of Grandpa Howard as a young man, with a man who might be Tennessee Williams."

She held the envelope out to Will and Tamara.

They looked at each other for a long moment. Finally, Will said, "You're the expert, Tamara. You're the one who'll have to authenticate it . . . or discredit it."

She swallowed. "I know." Looking at Natalie, she asked, "Are you sure you want to give this to me, Mrs. Drummond?

If I examine it, I'll probably be able to prove that your grandfather either imagined the whole thing or was deliberately lying about it."

"I know," Natalie said. "But I'm convinced he believed in it. If he was wrong, well, he didn't mean any harm by it. He just wanted to have created something lasting and important. I can understand that."

So could I. I suppose everybody has felt that way at one time or another. We all want to leave our mark on the world. One way or another, we all manage to do so, even though sometimes it's nothing more than a memory, and a smile on the face of someone who loves us.

And I think that matters a whole lot more than figuring out who wrote some dumb ol' play . . . don't you?

New Orleans and the
Tennessee Williams Literary Festival

For a quarter of a century, this annual festival in New Orleans has celebrated not only the lasting literary legacy of Thomas Lanier "Tennessee" Williams, but also that of Southern literature in general. Although I've taken a few liberties with the way the festival is scheduled and run (strictly for dramatic purposes, of course; I hope the subject of the festival would understand), for the most part, I've tried to present an accurate picture of this wonderful conference, as well as of the French Quarter, in which it takes place.

Each year, scholars and celebrities from all over the country gather in New Orleans for a series of discussions, lectures, presentations, and performances related to Tennessee Williams and other literary figures. The festival's website can be found at www.tennesseewilliams.net, where you can learn about the Friends of Tennessee, the organization that sponsors the festival, as well as other literary-oriented activities throughout the year.

The St. Emilion Hotel, in which most of this novel's action takes place, is fictional, although it's loosely based on the Bourbon Orleans, which serves as the host hotel for the Tennessee Williams Literary Festival (www.bourbonorleans.com). Petit Claude's, the jazz club where Delilah and her companions find Howard Burleson, is fictional as well, but New Orleans and especially the French Quarter have a long tradition of such clubs, dating back many years, such as the Famous Door, Dixie's Bar, and El Morocco. The Famous Door is still there (www.thebestofbourbonstreet.com), and the best-known jazz club currently operating is probably Preservation Hall (www.preservationhall.com), which has been in existence for almost fifty years. There are many other clubs that can be checked out at the tourism websites listed below. The café where Delilah and Will have dinner is based on the Louisiana Bistro (www.louisianabistro.net), one of the most highly rated restaurants in a city known all over the world for its wonderful food.

As for the French Quarter itself, as well as New Orleans in general, it remains one of the premier tourist destinations in the country. The website frenchquarter.com provides information about the history of this colorful area, as well as hotels, dining, nightlife, and other celebrations, such as Mardi Gras.

There's more to New Orleans than the French Quarter, of course, and to learn about the many attractions and opportunities the city offers to visitors, check out www.neworleanscvb.com, the website for the New Orleans Convention and Visitors Bureau, or www.neworleansonline.com, the city's official tourism website.

All the characters and incidents in this novel are entirely products of the author's imagination.